I0531497

Dakota Drudeson has been working for the Shifter Council for over fifty years. In all that time, he's believed that dragons—real dragons—either have never been real, or they'd died out centuries before. Imagine his surprise when his boss allows it to slip that dragons are alive, well, and there's even one working at Shifter Council Headquarters—a dishwasher named Charon, whom Dakota has always thought was human.

Watching Charon every chance he gets, Dakota quickly becomes infatuated with the small male. The fact that his boss has warned him that Charon's short, slender, blond frame isn't what he truly looks like doesn't concern him at all. Even the fact that the man's smell doesn't trigger interest from Dakota's Komodo dragon doesn't deter Dakota. He wants to earn Charon's trust and see his dragon.

Due to Dakota's promise to never reveal that he knows Charon is indeed a dragon, he can't even explain his odd obsession to his brothers. When Dakota finally gets his chance to admire Charon's gorgeous, metallic-purple dragon form, the man's true scent rocks him. Charon is his mate.

So when Dakota reveals himself, why doesn't Charon recognize him, too?

The unauthorized reproduction or distribution of this copyrighted work is illegal. Criminal copyright infringement, including infringement without monetary gain, is investigated by the FBI and is punishable by up to 5 years in federal prison and a fine of $250,000.

This book is a work of fiction. Names, characters, places, and incidents either are products of the author's imagination or are used fictitiously. Any resemblance to actual events or locales or persons, living or dead, is entirely coincidental.

Unveiling his Hidden Dragon
Copyright © 2022 Charlie Richards
ISBN: 978-1-4874-3629-2
Cover art by Angela Waters

All rights reserved. Except for use in any review, the reproduction or utilization of this work in whole or in part in any form by any electronic, mechanical or other means, now known or hereafter invented, is forbidden without the written permission of the publisher.

Published by eXtasy Books Inc

Look for us online at:
www.eXtasybooks.com

Unveiling his Hidden Dragon
Shifter's Regime 11

By

Charlie Richards

DEDICATION

To Family — the ones we're born into as well as the ones we make for ourselves.

CHAPTER ONE

"**W**hy are you staring at the kitchen doors? Miggs shouldn't be out with the cupcakes for another seven minutes."

Dakota Drudeson yanked his attention away from the double swinging doors. They led to the huge kitchens that pumped out food at Shifter Council Headquarters. Anyone who worked for or on the council had access to free meals there whenever they wished.

Considering shifters and other paranormals normally had pretty large appetites, Dakota knew that meant there were a number of people who worked in there.

Turning to look at his eldest brother, Delanrue—Del to family and close friends—Dakota knew the other Komodo dragon shifter referred to his Fate-given mate, Miggs—an uber-cute guinea pig shifter and the light of Del's life. He forced a smile and nodded, trying to figure out how to explain that the raspberry cupcakes Miggs was preparing for them, while delicious, were not what had his attention fixated on the kitchens. Instead, Dakota was trying to figure out a way to spot someone else, instead.

Charon.

Ever since taking a mission with his boss—Head Enforcer Mycroft—Dakota had become fascinated with the man. Mycroft had let it slip that Charon wasn't actually a human, even though he smelled like one. Instead, the lean blond was actually a dragon.

Like, a real one, not a Komodo dragon shifter like me.

Mycroft had also sworn him to secrecy.

Still, Dakota had never lied to his brother, and the uncomfortable prickle at the back of his neck told him that his silence felt like a lie by omission.

For the longest time — over one hundred sixty years — it had just been Dakota and his two brothers. It had been them against the world.

Their parents had been killed when he'd been young, and Del had raised him as well as Dane, their middle brother. While Dakota hadn't understood it at the time, Del had needed to grow up fast because their Komodo dragon bank hadn't been an exceptionally warm and fuzzy place.

It hadn't taken more than a few years before the dominance of Del's Komodo increased exponentially — probably due to his rising need to protect his younger brothers — and at a very young age — for a shifter, anyway — he'd earned the rank of enforcer.

Dakota knew that he hadn't been the only one with a case of hero worship on his big bro. He and Dane had discussed it a time or ten while growing up — about how badass Del was. When Del had moved from being an enforcer for their bank to being an enforcer for the Shifter Council, they'd worked hard to follow in his footsteps.

Of course, when Del transitioned to being an interrogator, they'd both congratulated him on his new position and wished him well. However, they hadn't been interested in that. That job required a certain type of personality, and they knew they didn't have it, and that was okay.

"Dakota?" Del rumbled, returning his attention to his brother. "Why are you staring at the doors?"

After another glance toward the double doors, Dakota focused on Del and admitted, "I'm actually hoping for a glimpse of Charon."

Del's eyes narrowed even as he managed to arch one eyebrow. "Charon," he repeated. "The little dishwasher?"

Dakota nodded. "Yeah."

While Mycroft had told Dakota that what everyone saw wasn't actually Charon's true form, he couldn't share that either. He hated keeping secrets from his brothers, but a promise was a promise. Dakota figured that trumped never keeping secrets from his brothers.

Wonder what he really looks like.

When Del narrowed his eyes even more, pinning Dakota with his intense stare, it took every bit of self-control Dakota possessed to keep from shifting uncomfortably in his seat . . . or opening his trap and blurting out the truth.

"Why?" Del asked as he relaxed back in his chair and crossed his arms over his chest.

Why indeed?

Dakota couldn't truly say for certain. Well, he knew part of it, anyway, but he couldn't share it with Del. He had been of the mind that dragons were either extinct or had never been real to begin with.

But I was wrong.

Now, Dakota desperately wanted to see one. To do that, he had to befriend Charon, then figure out how to earn his trust. Dakota figured, only then could he admit that he knew Charon was more than he seemed. Maybe after that, Dakota could convince the pretty man to show him his dragon.

Easy, right?

Except, Dakota had been trying to figure out how to meet Charon for several weeks. In all that time, he'd never seen the dishwasher exit the kitchen. He hadn't even been able to track him through the back corridors that he obviously used to get to and from his job.

Dakota had always thought Charon was human, and he didn't recall what the man's scent was. In order to track him, he would need to get close to Charon so he could get a real good lock on his smell. Then he could —

Wait a damn minute.

Jumping to his feet, Dakota grinned broadly at Del. "I think I'll go help Miggs carry the cupcakes."

Then Dakota strode briskly toward the kitchen doors.

Just as Dakota reached them, he felt a big hand clamp onto his shoulder. He turned, frowning. Seeing Del's narrow-eyed gaze, Dakota quickly morphed his features into a wide smile.

"Dakota, I know it's been a long time, but we discussed this," Del rumbled, his voice low and full of warning. "You don't shit where you work."

Dakota opened his mouth, then closed it again. "I'm not," he quickly assured. "I won't."

He understood his brother's concern. Sleeping with someone at work, someone not his fated mate, could make life extremely uncomfortable. While he thought Charon was cute, getting the man into bed wasn't his goal.

Even if the thought of it is damn tempting.

"Then what the hell is going through that head of yours?" Del demanded quietly, obviously trying to keep their conversation private. As Del squeezed Dakota's shoulder lightly, he added, "You've been squirrelly for a while, Dakota. What's up?"

Shit. I should have realized Del would notice.

His brother wasn't the top interrogator for nothing. He noticed things — facial tics, voice intonations, flicks of the eyes, and more — which others never picked up on. Mentally scrambling, Dakota swiftly thought about what to tell him.

"I'm being honest when I tell you I don't intend to seduce him," Dakota murmured, keeping his voice equally low. "But he has piqued my interest. No one ever sees him." Furrowing his brows, he felt a wash of sadness crash through him. "Doesn't that seem . . . lonely?"

"We don't know anything about him," Del pointed out. "He could have a wife and three kids that he rushes home to every day. This could just be a really good job for him, since he knows about us and the council pays extremely well."

Shrugging, Dakota claimed, "So, I'd like to find out." He smirked as he added, "You know what a friendly guy I am. I'm curious."

Del continued to stare at him — hard — for several heartbeats. Finally, he heaved a deep sigh before issuing a low growl. "I know you're hiding something, Dakota." Then his expression eased, and he slid his palm to cradle the back of Dakota's neck, giving it a light squeeze. "But you'll tell me when you're ready. Until then, we're here for you."

Dakota felt a wash of relief flood him. "Thanks, Del."

Never could he feel grateful enough to know that he would always have his brothers at his back . . . even when they didn't know what they might be helping him with.

"Well, let's go see if he's here, then," Del muttered, leading the way into the kitchen.

Dakota followed his brother. He panned his gaze around the massive, industrial-sized space. While Del barely cast a glance toward the back where the cleaning area was situated, Dakota's attention remained riveted in that direction.

There, unloading a dishwasher, worked Charon.

Slowing his steps, Dakota lagged behind Del as he watched the man. The five-foot-six or seven guy appeared to be lithe, although it was tough to tell, considering the tan, nondescript slacks and loose polo shirt he wore. His rolled-up sleeves showcased lightly muscled, pale limbs.

As if sensing that someone watched him, Charon stiffened, his shoulders tightening. He straightened and peered over his shoulder. His blue-eyed gaze met Dakota's. For an instant, Charon just stared at him. Then a faint flush pinkened the man's cheeks, and he quickly ducked his head, turned back to the waiting dishwasher, and grabbed a stack of dishes before hurrying to a cupboard to put them away.

To Dakota's surprise, a punch of interest that had nothing to do with curiosity warmed his belly. A low level of arousal warmed his gut.

Well, huh.

Recalling his exchange with Del, Dakota yanked his attention away from Charon.

Just friends.

Dakota focused on Del, who stood behind Miggs. He had his hands resting on his much smaller mate's hips, and he nuzzled the side of the guinea pig shifter's neck with his lips. Considering Del stood six-foot-five and Miggs was a diminutive five-foot-one, Dakota thought it looked awkward as hell.

Seeing the happy expressions on both men's faces, even as Miggs continued to focus on frosting the cupcakes, Dakota knew that neither man minded any contortions they had to do to make it work.

As Dakota watched Miggs slather frosting on the last cupcake, he noticed how Miggs's hand shook a little, obviously affected by Del's attentions. Rubbing at his chest, Dakota glanced away. Still not used to seeing his brother act so intimately with another, Dakota felt as if he was interrupting an intimate moment.

Out of the corner of his eye, Dakota spotted Charon standing on his toes, reaching up while holding a stack of plates. He saw the way the man struggled to get the plates on top of the stack, wobbling a little. His body even appeared to tremble.

Unable to help himself, Dakota hurried to Charon's side. He reached past him, damn near bracketing him, and gripped the stack on either side. While Dakota helped slip the plates on top of the stack, he kept his body away from the other man's, even though he felt so tempted to find out what it would feel like to press against him.

Friends. Damn it.

Dakota quickly stepped back, saying, "Sorry to startle you,

Charon." When the man turned and eyed him warily, Dakota quickly added, "You just looked like you needed a hand."

Charon's big blue eyes narrowed. "How do you know my name?"

Surprised upon hearing the defensiveness in his tone, Dakota lifted his hands in placation, palms out. "Uh, I'm a Council Enforcer." He lowered his left hand to his side as he touched his chest with the fingertips of his right. "Dakota. Dakota Drudeson." Dakota grinned widely. "Most of us know the names of just about everyone who works here and can recognize them by sight." With a wink, he told him, "Gotta know everyone so if someone's here that shouldn't be, we can spot them."

Slowly, Charon nodded, although his eyes remained narrowed. "Okay."

Dakota rested his hands on his hips, continuing to smile at him. "You knooooooow." He purposefully drew the words out, adding playfulness to his tone. "I'm not certain who or what dragged you into the paranormal world, but we're not all bastards."

Dakota kept his words as true as he could, just in case the man could scent, well, not lies, but a stretch of the truth. After all, he had no idea what kind of abilities a dragon actually had. Dakota knew that the dragon believed that everyone — well, probably everyone save Mycroft and those on the council — thought he was a human.

Keeping a winning smile creasing his lips, Dakota added, "You don't have to hide from us."

Cocking his head, Charon asked, "What makes you think I'm hiding from you?"

Dakota did a quick think of his possible responses and decided on, "Well, you rarely enter the dining hall to eat lunch or during a break." After all, he'd been watching for the last several weeks. "And you must use the back hallways to get to and from your job here in the kitchens." Offering a shrug, Dakota told him, "If you had a bad experience with someone here, if you don't want to tell me, share it with your boss. I happen to know Chef Gage is a pretty decent guy, and he always has the best interest of his people at heart."

On more than one occasion, Dakota had met up with Chef Gage—a very nice and happy to help cinnamon-colored black bear—to get pointers on cooking to help him on dates. Just because he knew that person wasn't his fated mate didn't mean he didn't want to treat that person right.

"You know Chef Gage?" Charon cocked his head. "Really?"

"Surprised?" Dakota chuckled as he shrugged. "I happen to enjoy cooking and learning new dishes, and he's an excellent teacher."

Charon didn't appear to believe him, making Dakota wonder why.

Surely a dragon can tell if a shifter is lying or not.

"Well, I'm not hiding from anyone," Charon claimed, his scent declaring that he spoke the truth. "I do my job and go home." He shrugged as his gaze slid to the left. "Always stuff to do at home."

While Dakota could smell that Charon continued to speak the truth, there was something else in there, too . . . something that gave a subtle flavor indicating he might be hiding something as well.

Dakota reined in his natural tendency to push. He was trying to win Charon's trust, after all.

"Well, glad to hear it," Dakota began, racking his brain for something to say that would extend the conversation.

"Hey, Dakota," Miggs interrupted. "Hi, Charon."

"Miggs," Charon replied with a nod. "Well, I better get back to work."

To Dakota's dismay, Charon began to turn away, heading back toward the dishwasher he'd obviously been emptying.

Dakota forced a smile as he eyed Miggs, his expression relaxing when he took in the tray of cupcakes the small shifter held. "Damn, Miggs. Those look good."

"Um, yeah. Thanks," Miggs replied.

That was when Dakota noted Miggs's flushed face and the hungry gleam in Del's eyes, not to mention the aroma of lust that superseded the smell of the raspberry cupcakes.

"You can take them." Miggs held out the tray. "Me and Del are just gonna take a couple and head to our suite."

Each shifter who worked as an enforcer or councilman had a private suite at headquarters, and Dakota could easily guess what the pair were more interested in.

"Okay. Thanks."

After Dakota took the tray, Miggs grabbed four cupcakes, then turned away. "Talk to you later," he stated with a smile.

Del didn't even bother saying good-bye. He just wrapped his arm around his mate's shoulders and hurried him out of the kitchen.

With an idea percolating in his mind, Dakota turned toward Charon. "Hey, Charon." Once he had the blond's attention, he held up the tray. "Come have a cupcake with me."

CHAPTER TWO

Pulling on a pair of jeans, Charon wondered how Dakota had convinced him to agree to go to the barbeque.

Right. The Komodo dragon shifter is incredibly charismatic.

Charon had to admit that the big blond was super easy on the eyes, too. As he buttoned and zipped his jeans, he pushed that thought from his mind. He'd known who Dakota was even before he'd introduced himself, and he knew about his reputation as a bit of a player. Charon shouldn't want to become just another one of his conquests.

Although, Dakota didn't really seem to be interested in me like that.

Charon tried not to feel too much disappointment in that.

After agreeing to eat a couple of cupcakes with Dakota — they had looked and smelled delicious, after all — Charon had sat with the shifter in the cafeteria. He'd felt self-conscious as hell, having rarely ventured into the area if it wasn't required by his work. If the kitchens were busy, Charon occasionally had to bus tables when there was a run on jerks who didn't bother returning their trays to the drop-off window.

Unable to help himself, Charon had hummed appreciatively at the taste of the raspberry cupcake — it even had raspberry filling — and Dakota had laughed and told him, "If you think this is good, you should try his angel food cake. It's beyond amazing."

Without thought, Charon had admitted, "I've never had angel food cake."

Dakota had pinned him with a scandalized expression.

"What?" he'd gasped. "Never?"

For the first time in . . . in Charon couldn't remember, he found himself chuckling. "Never."

"Oh, that's it." Dakota shook his head and pulled out his phone. "I'm asking Miggs to make one for the barbeque I'm throwing for Dane, welcoming him and Danny back from their honeymoon." Continuing to text, Dakota kept glancing at Charon. "Say you'll come. You have to have some." Grinning, Dakota had added, "Bring the wife and kids, too. There's always more than enough food." Then he'd sobered and leaned toward him. "Uh, do they know about paranormals, too? We'll need to know if we need to watch what we say and shit."

Charon had bit back a snort at how earnest the shifter appeared. "Uh, no. No wife or kids."

After a little more coaxing—plus showing Charon his phone with Miggs's confirmation that he would indeed make the angel food cake—Charon had agreed to attend.

Then Dakota had grinned broadly and asked, "Great. What's your number? I'll text you my address."

He'd hesitated a few seconds, then given the man his number.

A second later, he'd felt his phone vibrate in his pocket as Dakota declared, "And now you have mine." He pointed at the tray containing several more cupcakes. "You wanna take a couple of these home with you?"

Charon had, so he took them.

After Dakota had said his good-bye, and Charon had tucked the cupcakes into his locker, he'd begun to wonder just what the hell had happened.

Days later, Charon couldn't figure out how he'd ended up on Dakota's radar. He did his job, reported to Mycroft—the Shifter Council's head enforcer, so he could report back to his people—and pretty much tried to stay out of everyone else's way. For almost a decade, that hadn't changed.

So why now?

Charon wondered if the changes to the magick binding him might be the answer. He could feel it . . . and so could his dragon. The spells holding him trapped in this human form had weakened enough for him to even manage a partial shift.

Has my scent changed?

Except, Charon didn't think that made sense. Dakota and everyone else he came into contact with still treated him like the human he'd always presented to be. Surely Mycroft would have mentioned a change like that.

Dismissing the idea, Charon returned to getting ready for the barbeque, choosing a green polo shirt from his closet. He'd tried to figure out a way to get out of going, but his nature wouldn't allow him to. As an omega dragon, Charon's word was his bond, so if he said he would do something, he needed to get it done.

And that's exactly how I ended up in this mess.

Charon's father had always warned him to watch what he said. He had, too . . . until he'd become so angry at Elder Gaithnos's insistent urgings that he forge a mate-bond with his son, Glindber. Charon didn't even like the male. In fact, he disliked Glindber and his overbearing attitude, and he certainly didn't want to spend any more time with him than he had to.

The last time Gaithnos had nearly cornered Charon and ordered him to bond with Glindber, he'd angrily—and flippantly—replied, "I'd rather be dead than bond with your asshole son." It hadn't helped that Charon had already been having a bad day, but he really should have known better.

Gaithnos's beady brown eyes had narrowed, and a malicious smile had curved his thin lips. "Oh, you won't be dead, but you'll wish you were, Charon." Then the elder had turned and stalked away.

Charon hadn't known what Gaithnos meant until he'd

been called before King Leortis three days later. He still remembered that moment clearly, as if it had happened just the prior day.

"Hey, where are you going?" Borath called, frowning at Charon as he hurried past him on the garden pathway.

Pausing for a second — after all, while Charon considered Borath a friend, he was still technically his boss — he showed him the scroll a messenger had handed him the moment before. "I've been summoned by King Leortis," Charon told him, unease churning in his gut.

Borath scanned the scroll quickly before the larger male pinned him with a wide-eyed stare. "Damn." He returned the scroll to Charon as he asked, "What the hell did you do?"

Charon shook his head. "I haven't done anything." Furrowing his brows, he racked his brain even as he came up empty . . . again. "Certainly nothing that would draw the attention of the king." Glancing around uneasily at the expanse of neatly trimmed hedges that made up the intricate garden maze, Charon murmured, "Everything is neat and trimmed and blooming nicely. Even the chrysanthemums are starting to flourish again."

They'd had a problem with beetles destroying them, but the gardening team had caught it before they'd completely killed them.

"It's never good to be summoned," Borath muttered, shaking his head. "Good luck."

"Thanks," Charon murmured, turning to continue on his way. "I hope it doesn't take too long." Worry filled him. "I still need to weed the south garden."

Borath patted him on the shoulder. "You never rush the king. If I don't see you back here within an hour, I'll have Kulrath do it."

Even as Charon nodded and headed down the path, he internally winced. Kulrath wouldn't be happy about that. The older blue dragon always complained that it bothered his knees.

Charon quickly traversed the palace hallways. When he reached the entrance to the throne room, he paused and took a deep breath, hoping for a little courage. As he lifted his hand to knock, a guard approached.

"You're Charon, aren't you?"

Surprised that the uniformed dragon knew him, Charon nodded quickly. "Yes, sir."

"The king is waiting for you in the small receiving room." The guard frowned. "Didn't the messenger tell you?"

Uh, had the messenger said that?

No. Definitely not.

Charon shook his head. "No, sir. He just gave me this scroll, told me it was urgent, and hurried off."

The guard frowned even as he jerked his chin in a single nod. Then he turned and beckoned. "This way."

Following silently, Charon sure hoped he hadn't just gotten the guy into trouble. He didn't want to cause someone else problems, even if he had screwed up.

As Charon neared the small receiving room, a slither of fear worked its way up his spine.

The small receiving room. Why would King Leortis want to speak to me in such an intimate setting?

An idea flashed into his mind . . . one that Charon really hoped didn't come to pass.

King Leortis used the small receiving room to discuss arranging mate-bonds between two parties.

After the guard knocked twice and the king's deep voice called for them to enter, the man opened the door and led the way inside.

"Ah, thank you, Enforcer Karnak." King Leortis rose from

where he'd been sitting behind a large desk and began rounding it. "So, this is young Charon."

"It is, Sire."

Upon hearing the slightly nasal voice, Charon snapped his attention to the left. He spotted Elder Gaithnos standing off to the side, and his gut clenched. Upon seeing the malicious sneer curving the elder's lips when their gazes met, Charon felt a bead of sweat trickle down his back.

When King Leortis glanced Elder Gaithnos's way, the nasty look was gone to be replaced by a bland smile.

King Leortis slowly crossed to Charon, stopping ten feet in front of him. "It's unorthodox to send an omega dragon for this assignment, but Elder Gaithnos assures me you'd prefer it over breeding."

"I-I . . . u-um . . ." Charon stammered, confused beyond words.

To Charon's surprise, King Leortis smiled in a sort-of . . . fatherly way. "Relax, Charon." He chuckled softly as he moved closer. "Not all omega dragons want to breed as soon as they hit their majority."

Charon knew King Leortis referred to when a dragon reached one hundred years of age. Except, he'd just reached ninety. He didn't understand what that had to do with anything.

King Leortis rested his hand on Charon's shoulder, his gaze appearing understanding. "While your kind are rare and valued amongst our people, I would never force you to breed if that isn't what you wish." Then his features eased into a serious expression—solemn even. "With that said, I don't have a problem with you taking over the position of Liaison to the Shifter Council when it opens in a week, but because you're an omega, certain . . . precautions will have to be put into place."

"L-Liaison to—" Charon couldn't even get the words out.

He was just too shocked.

What the hell?

Nodding, King Leortis squeezed his shoulder gently, then used the hold to turn him toward the sofas arranged on the left side of the room as a sitting or lounge area. The king guided him onto a nicely padded chair before relaxing on the sofa to the left. Elder Gaithnos settled on a sofa to the right, keeping plenty of space between them.

"So, because we don't want you accidentally getting knocked up by some random shifter or human"—King Leortis lifted a hand, palm out, in placation as he glanced toward Elder Gaithnos—"the elder's words, but he's right. Anyway, we'll need to be-spell you when you're in human form so you'll actually *be* human." The king smiled wryly as he stated, "Normal human men can't get pregnant."

Unable to go against King Leortis's orders, Charon sat in shocked silence as he listened to him and Elder Gaithnos plan the next phase of his life.

Snapping out of the memory, Charon returned to the here and now. Over the years, he often wondered if King Leortis had known that when he'd sent Charon with Elder Gaithnos and a guard that he wasn't just making him human in human form. Instead, Gaithnos had ordered the aging wizard dragon, whose job it was to be-spell him, to bind Charon's dragon form, too, forcing him to stay human all the time.

The old wizard dragon had shrugged his boney shoulders, focused watery, pale-blue eyes on Charon, and begun to chant.

As few wizard dragons existed—and they were the only ones with the power to cast a spell on a fellow dragon—Charon had never experienced the effects of a spell. After his century of servitude to the Shifter Council, he hoped never to again. While he felt the spell's effects weakening, Charon didn't know what it meant, and he was far too afraid to ask anyone.

What if word somehow finds its way back to Elder Gaithnos?

Charon had heard tales of the elder's vindictiveness, which explained why he had to work as a lowly dishwasher to the shifters even as he completed his liaison duties . . . and why very few were authorized to know of what he actually was— a dragon. If he weaseled out of the male's punishment for rejecting his son, even partly, what else would he try? Charon didn't want to find out.

I'll serve my hundred years. In the meantime, I'll find a way to avoid returning to the palace after I'm finished. Surely there are other places that need the talents of a gardener.

Charon missed working outside almost as much as he missed flying.

Pushing away thoughts of things he couldn't change, Charon slipped his arms into a light jacket and grabbed his keys. He headed to his open-topped *Jeep*, grateful for the mild spring weather. Feeling the wind blowing through his hair was as close as he'd found to soaring across the skies.

With a sigh, Charon fired up his *Jeep* and headed out of his garage. He checked his GPS and followed its directions. Charon noticed he was headed toward the north edge of town where homes were placed on large lots that backed to forest.

As jealousy twisted in his gut, Charon knew the space would be lost on him, since he still couldn't take his true form.

Hopefully soon, though.

Charon would keep trying. The partial shift he'd successfully accomplished the prior weekend had renewed his hope.

Someday . . . Someday soon.

When Charon spotted the address Dakota had given him, he had to follow the driveway through the trees and around a bend. He whistled under his breath when the home came into view. The large A-frame structure was situated to face toward the rear of the property with huge windows that probably gave a fantastic view of the trees.

A large, sprawling deck had been built in front and around the side to the right, disappearing from view.

Several other vehicles were parked in front of the two-car garage situated to the home's left. Inside the open bay door were three motorcycles — two large road-style bikes and one bullet bike.

As Charon parked, his focus lingered on the metallic purple racing bike, wondering what the wind in his hair would feel like on that thing. He'd never learned to drive one, as no one in his circle had used them, and he hadn't wanted to be taught by a human — prejudiced probably, but oh well. Staring at the gorgeous machine, he found himself rethinking his decision. Maybe if he was taught by a shifter, his dragon nature of thinking he was better than others wouldn't get in the way.

Hell, I've been doing their dishes for almost ten years. How bad could it be?

After shutting off his engine, Charon could hear the sounds of men laughing and chatting somewhere out of sight. He swallowed hard as a pang of loneliness stabbed through his chest. Rubbing at it absently, Charon took a few slow deep breaths.

Once the sensation had eased, Charon grabbed the bottle of wine and the box of beer he'd left in his *Jeep* earlier that day and exited his vehicle.

I can do this. I can play human with Dakota and a bunch of shifters.

And maybe, it'll ease some of this loneliness I constantly feel.

CHAPTER THREE

"Why do you keep looking toward the front of the house?" Dane asked curiously, following Dakota's line of sight. "You can't see it through the trees, anyway."

Dakota bit back a frustrated growl, knowing Dane was right. Smiling at his middle brother, he shrugged. "Just waiting for Charon to show up." Dakota checked his phone for what had to be the millionth time, just in case he'd missed a call or text from the man.

Nope.

Dane narrowed his eyes as he gazed at Dakota. "If I didn't know any better, I'd say you have a crush on the human."

Shaking his head, Dakota immediately denied that. "Naw, bro." He punched his brother's upper arm playfully. "Just tryin' to get him out into the world. It's like he's totally alone."

"How do you know that?" Dane asked, cocking his head and eyeing him askance. "You've talked to him . . . what? Once?"

Dakota cleared his throat as he shrugged. "Well, yeah," he admitted. "In person anyway. We've been exchanging texts since Tuesday."

While that was a bit of a stretch, Dakota wouldn't admit it. In truth, he would always have to text Charon first. The dragon never initiated their conversations.

"Is Charon your mate?" Dane asked bluntly, crossing his arms over his chest.

"No," Dakota stated, fighting back a bit of sadness. "I think I would have noticed before now."

Dane nodded slowly. "Okay, well, you know Del's rule."

"I know," Dakota confirmed. "Don't shit where you work." Raising his hands in placation, he told Dane, "He's already reminded me."

Nodding once more, Dane opened his mouth, only to snap it closed again. He jerked his chin upward just a smidge, indicating something behind Dakota.

Dakota turned, but he already knew what he would see. The hairs that stood on his nape gave it away. Upon spotting a slowly approaching Charon, Dakota felt his gut tighten as if butterflies were taking up residence.

Damn. Why am I suddenly reacting to this guy? My Komodo has zero interest in him.

Chalking it up to his fascination with seeing Charon's true form, Dakota grinned at Charon. "Hey, Charon," he greeted, taking a few steps toward him while waving. "Glad you found the place." Dakota lifted a hand, intending to reach for Charon. Realizing what he was doing, he quickly pivoted a half-turn and used that hand to indicate his brother. "Just in case you've never been formally introduced, this is my brother, Dane."

Charon dipped his head a little as he murmured, "Enforcer Dane."

Dane held out his hand, saying, "No titles here, Charon." As Charon slowly reached out and gripped Dane's hand, returning the handshake, Dane added, "Out here, we're just a bunch of guys hanging out enjoying good food and company."

Dakota had no idea why he suddenly felt like growling at Dane.

Surely it doesn't take that long to shake his hand. And holy shit. What the hell am I thinking?

Knowing he really needed to get his head out of his ass, Dakota offered, "Can I get you a drink?" As they began moving toward the others gathered on the deck and the tables set up amidst the trees, Dakota peered at the bottle of white wine and twelve-pack of beer Charon carried. "I can open that wine for you, or I can check to see what's already opened. Miggs drinks red, but I know I have a white open, too."

Snapping his mouth shut, Dakota spotted the slight twitch of Dane's brow as his brother glanced his way before turning to fall into step with the pair of them. He wanted to roll his eyes at himself. Dakota couldn't remember the last time he'd rambled.

Good grief.

"Uh, I'm good with whatever white you have open," Charon told him, glancing from Dakota's face to peer around the group. He paused an instant, nearly tripping, before continuing forward. "Is that Councilman Colearian?" Charon's eyes widened. "And several other councilmen?"

Dakota chuckled as he nodded. "Yeah. Since Councilman Shane Alvaro joined their ranks" — he jerked his chin in the direction of a dark-haired wolf shifter — "and started monthly poker nights, several of the councilmen have begun hanging out in a more relaxed setting."

"Huh." Charon cocked his head and muttered, "How come I didn't know that?"

Dakota opened his mouth, then closed it again, uncertain how to respond to that. He didn't know why Charon would know about it. Then he realized that perhaps it was something that Charon probably thought he should pass on to his dragon peers.

Damn. I wish I could ask. There are so many things I want to ask.

Unfortunately, Dakota knew he couldn't.

Hopefully soon.

Evidently, Charon realized he'd spoken out loud, for he quickly cleared his throat and lifted the box of beer. "You mentioned in a text that you enjoy sampling different local microbrews. This is one I like, so—" Charon snapped his mouth shut, his cheeks taking on a pinkish hue as his obvious embarrassment perfumed the air.

Dakota thought the man's gesture was damn sweet. Grinning, he took the box and read the label. "Thank, man." He nudged his elbow into Charon's upper arm, making the guy rock sideways. "I haven't tried this one, yet." Opening the box with his free hand, Dakota reached inside and pulled out a can. "Want one?"

Offering it to Dane, his brother shrugged and took it. "Sure."

After pulling out another, Dakota held it out to Charon. "You brought it. You want?"

Charon lifted his free hand, palm out, as he shook his head. "Not interested tonight." He held up the bottle of wine. "I'm in the mood for wine tonight."

"Got it." Dakota tucked the box under his arm, freeing his hand to pop the top on the can. "Come over to the sliding doors. That's where the drink table is set up." As Dakota led the way, he took a sip of the brew. After swirling the carbonated alcohol over his tongue, he hummed and swallowed. "Pretty good." Seeing Dane doing something similar, he asked, "What do you think?"

Dane winced and shook his head. "I don't think I'll be switching brands anytime soon."

Dakota laughed, pleased when Charon at least chuckled softly, telling him he was beginning to loosen up a bit.

Del glanced their way from where he was manning the grill. His gaze slid over them, pausing on the beer Dane held. "That's not your usual."

Holding out the can, Dane offered, "Charon brought it. Wanna try it?"

After setting down the tongs he held, Del took the beer and swigged a mouthful. He grunted as he swallowed. "Good." Then he held it back out to Dane.

Taking a step backward, Dane lifted his hands in surrender. "Ah, keep it." He turned toward the drinks table, saying, "I think I'll get my usual."

Del shrugged and took another drink. Then he set it beside the tongs, as well as an already opened bottle of beer, before picking up the tongs while asking, "You a hotdog or burger guy, Charon?"

"Uh, I like both," Charon replied.

As Del asked him how he liked them—dog burned or not, burger with cheese or no—Dakota turned his attention to the drinks table. He placed the box of beer on the deck beneath the table and his open can on top of it. After choosing a wine glass, Dakota grabbed the open white wine from the bucket of ice and filled the glass before putting it back.

Dakota picked it up and moved back to Charon's side, where—to his surprise—he was discussing grilling techniques with Del. At a lull in the conversation, Dakota offered the glass. "How about I trade you?"

Charon smiled a little as he took the glass and handed over the bottle. "Thanks."

Nodding, Dakota tried to think of something to say, but he came up empty.

"Hey, Charon," Mycroft greeted, joining them near the grill. "Glad to see you here." He cast a pointed look Dakota's way while Charon was taking a sip of wine before clearing his expression and adding, "Didn't realize you and Dakota were acquainted."

After swallowing, his Adam's apple bobbing slightly, Charon admitted, "Just met recently." He shoved his empty hand into his pocket while rocking on his feet a bit as he muttered, "Uh, he promised me angel food cake."

"Enjoy angel food cake?" Mycroft responded with a grin. "Didn't realize you had a sweet tooth."

"I don't," Charon replied. Then he cleared his throat and

quickly added, "Um, have a sweet tooth, I mean." With a shrug, he admitted, "And I've never had it, so was interested in trying it."

Mycroft nodded as he turned his piercing, green-eyed gaze on Dakota. "Is Miggs making it?"

Dakota grinned broadly. "Yup. I asked him special."

The corners of Mycroft's lips curved into a small smile. "Well, you can't go wrong with that. Miggs's angel food cake is delicious."

"My mate makes amazing baked goods," Del cut in proudly, his chest puffing up. "I didn't have a sweet tooth before, but I damn sure do now." Dakota's eldest brother smirked. "And I'm damn grateful for my shifter metabolism."

"Me, too," Dakota quipped. He just caught himself before nudging Charon and proclaiming, right? Instead, he asked, "Is that food about done, Del?"

"Yup," Del replied. After taking a swig of beer, he used the can to point toward the house. "Get me a platter. I forgot it."

Dakota lifted his own can in a mock salute. "Be right back."

Hurrying into the house, Dakota couldn't help glancing behind him. He spotted Mycroft pat Charon on the shoulder before heading toward the drinks table. As Dakota reached into a cupboard, he craned his neck to see out his kitchen window, continuing to watch the dragon in human form.

"You know, I'm beginning to think you're a stalker."

Flinching upon hearing Dane's voice, Dakota nearly dropped the platter he'd just pulled from the cupboard. He spun, finding his brother leaning one shoulder against the wall. Dane had his arms crossed over his chest, one ankle crossed over the other, and a speculative look on his face.

"Shit, man," Dakota grumbled. "What the hell?"

"You tell me," Dane countered, narrowing his eyes. "And the truth would be good, this time."

Realizing he had to share something, Dakota groaned as he

tipped his head back and stared at the ceiling. "I—" He paused a few heartbeats, and when Dane didn't comment or move, he heaved a deep breath. Resting his butt against the kitchen counter, Dakota crossed his arms, tucking the platter within them. After a quick glance around, confirming they were alone, Dakota lowered his voice and murmured, "I found out something fascinating about Charon, but I can't tell you because I was sworn to secrecy." When Dane frowned, appearing unconvinced, Dakota added, "It's true, and yeah, now I've become a little obsessed with the guy." Unwinding one arm, he scrubbed his fingers through his hair. "I . . . I can't explain it better than that."

Pursing his lips, Dane tipped his head to the side and cracked his neck. His eyes were narrowed, and his expression appeared a little vacant. Even his nostrils flared, telling Dakota that his brother was openly scenting him, probably trying to figure him out.

Dakota knew he couldn't say more. With a sigh, he lifted the platter and stated, "Del is waiting." Then he headed out of the kitchen.

Dane gripped Dakota's upper arm, pausing him as he passed. "I'm worried about you, brother," he murmured. "Be careful." As Dane released him, he added, "And you know I'm here for you if you need anything."

"I know, Dane," Dakota replied, smiling at his brother. He felt warmed inside by Dane's concern, his words nearly mirroring Del's. Dakota knew that, no matter what, his brothers had his back. "And I'll be careful, and once I figure this shit out with Charon, you and Del will be the first to know."

Nodding, Dane patted his back. "Let's get that platter to Del." Arching one brow as he started toward the sliding glass door, he added, "And perhaps save Charon from Rigel's dubious attentions."

Dakota followed Dane's line of sight and growled under

his breath, the heat of anger surging through him. Fellow enforcer Rigel Patterson—an alligator shifter—stood beside Charon. He was grinning widely as he lifted the bottle of white wine and poured more into Charon's glass.

"Don't act jealous," Dane rumbled into his ear. "You have no rights to him."

"Shit," Dakota muttered, grabbing the handle of the sliding door. "I know you're right. So why the fuck do I want to tug Charon away from Rigel or bash the player's head in?"

While the Drudeson brothers had always kept to their policy of not hooking up with people who could be considered their co-workers, even if they worked in different departments, Rigel didn't hold to that policy. Dakota could think of dozens of liaisons that he'd learned of either through scent when working with the shifter or the grapevine sharing tales of his conquests or angry scorned lovers. Considering Rigel's antics weren't the only ones added to the gossip mill, Dakota had always had an easy time of staying away from others working at the Shifter Council, no matter how much they flirted.

"Keep your head about you, Dakota," Dane encouraged, squeezing the back of his neck as he moved past his brother. "No knocking out another enforcer over something you haven't figured out, yet."

Keeping his brother's words firmly in mind, Dakota pasted a smile on his face as he headed to the grill, taking the platter to Del.

Too bad that took him farther away from where Charon and Rigel were standing.

I'll keep an eye on things from a distance. I did tell my brothers that I thought he needed friends.

Rigel had just better not get too friendly.

Pushing the errant thoughts away, Dakota held the platter while Del loaded it with food.

CHAPTER FOUR

Hearing his phone chime, Charon picked it up and smiled. *Barbeque at Dane's Saturday. The house on the other side of me — not Del's side.*

Charon quickly texted back with a *thumbs up* emoji as he grinned. He didn't have any family, so he found Dakota and his brother's setup fascinating. The brothers all lived right next to each other — Del to Dakota's right, and Dane to the left. Each had a plot of a couple dozen acres, and they backed up to property owned by one of the councilmen, so they could shift and run at will.

If I could shift, that would be a wonderfully secluded place to do it.

After tucking his phone into his back pocket, Charon returned to work, still smiling. He couldn't remember the last time he'd had a standing invitation to hang with people. Even when Charon had worked as a gardener at King Leortis's estate, he'd only had a small circle of friends — himself and three others — but they'd been busy with their own lives, only getting together a couple of times a month.

Dakota's group — his brothers, their mates, and a number of other enforcers and even a few councilmen and their partners — had welcomed Charon with open arms. He hadn't realized how much he'd missed spending time with people until he'd started again. While he still feared his activities would get back to Elder Gaithnos, he decided he couldn't allow the vindictive dragon to continue running his life.

I allowed him to do just that for too long.

27

When Charon had begun working at Shifter Headquarters, he hadn't taken into consideration how different shifter culture was compared to dragon culture. If a human wasn't mated with a dragon, they were pretty much ignored or considered second-class citizens. Although, Charon had heard that—now that King Leortis had found his mate in a human, as had a few others—that was beginning to change.

Shifters didn't seem to care in the least that Charon was a human—or that he presented as one. They laughed and joked with him, tempering their strength so they didn't hurt him when they patted him on the back or nudged his arm.

Charon's favorite times were when Dakota companionably slung his arm around his shoulders. It caused his gut to clench and his arms to goose bump. Even his skin heated, and he had to fight back a blush.

Except, never once had Dakota made any indication that he was interested in Charon for more than friendship.

Too bad. I'd have loved to break my dry spell by engaging in a romp with him.

Charon knew there were a couple of others that would help him out with that. Enforcer Rigel had made his interest clear. While Charon felt tempted to take the handsome alligator shifter up on his offer, something held him back.

Guess I don't want to get laid that bad, yet.

"Who are you mooning over?"

Upon hearing Desmond's question, Charon realized he was still smiling. He sobered as he shook his head. "Not mooning over anyone," he countered.

"And the smile is gone." Desmond sighed as he walked past him to grab a mixing bowl. "You've smelled a lot happier lately. Just thought maybe you'd met someone."

"Smelled happier?" Charon murmured, eyeing the slender, red fox shifter as he continued to rinse dishes before loading them into the dishwasher. "I guess I have been happier."

"So, what's changed?" Desmond leaned his hip against the

counter, cradling the bowl in his arms. "If you don't mind my asking." He smiled wryly. "I guess I am being a little nosey, seeing as we don't normally talk." Then Desmond's brows furrowed. "Um, I don't really see you talk to anyone."

"I got invited to a barbeque by Dakota a couple of weekends ago," Charon admitted. He knew Desmond was a nice guy. He'd even overheard him offering a polar bear shifter advice about proper ways to refer to gay men. "I've been to a couple of them now, and he and his buddies are all really nice." After licking his lips, Charon told the shifter, "I didn't realize that shifters accepted humans into their circle. Um, that's why I've been keeping to myself."

Scoffing, Desmond rolled his eyes. "I don't know who told you that, but it's so not true." He cocked his head. "Uh, hanging with Dakota and his crowd, huh? They're a good bunch of guys. Fun to hang with."

"How come I haven't seen you there?" Charon grimaced. "Um, that was rude. Sorry."

Desmond pushed away from the counter as he barked a laugh. "Don't worry about it. I get messages from Dane about when and where they are, but I can't always make it." As he headed toward the counter to start making . . . something . . . he explained, "My mom occasionally needs help around the house, especially in the spring." As Desmond placed the bowl on the counter and began pulling out ingredients—if Charon had to guess, he thought it was batter for waffles—he continued, "After hours of yard work last weekend, I was tired and didn't feel like going out. The weekend before, I fixed a plumbing problem." Grimacing, he shook his head. "After that, all I wanted was a long hot shower."

Charon winced in sympathy. "That's definitely one of the things I like about renting a condo," he admitted. "The building management has to take care of stuff like that."

Humming, Desmond nodded, too. "I hear that." He

shrugged before admitting, "But my fox wouldn't like that very much. No privacy."

As Charon nodded in understanding, he knew that if he could return to his true form, he would feel the strain, too.

Huh. If I do successfully shift, then I might have to think about moving. Except, would that be a dead giveaway to anyone watching me?

"Something troubling just entered your mind," Desmond commented, peering at him as he whisked the batter. "Is everything okay?"

"Yeah, yeah," Charon quickly assured. "Maybe I'll see you Saturday, then?"

Desmond nodded slowly, probably knowing Charon changed the subject on purpose, but the fox shifter let it go.

Charon returned his attention to his duties. As he worked, he ignored most everyone in favor of dwelling on his thoughts.

To his surprise, Charon had noticed that the more time he spent with the shifters, the more he could feel his dragon form unfurling within him. He wondered if being in the vicinity of so many dominant males was triggering his body's need to be in the form best suited to defending himself. While Charon knew that none of Dakota's friends would injure him purposefully, his instincts still warred within him—especially when Rigel or a couple of others hit on him.

As Charon finished putting away the pots he'd just washed and dried, he glanced toward the clock, checking the time.

Time to go.

Once Charon had put away the last item, he called a goodbye to Desmond, getting a wave and a, "See you tomorrow," in return.

Charon pushed through the door that led from the kitchen to the back room. Crossing to his locker, he spun the dial on the combination lock, entering the numbers needed to open it. After it'd clicked open, Charon reached in and grabbed his jacket.

Just as Charon pulled on his second sleeve, he felt the hairs on his nape stand on end. He paused just long enough to half-zip his jacket before turning. Rigel stood just inside the door, talking to another man.

While Rigel appeared relaxed, resting most of his weight on his left foot, the other guy's eyes were narrowed as he eyed Rigel when the alligator shifter asked, "Are you lost, man?"

The dark-haired stranger shook his head. "No. Just exploring," he claimed. His gaze slid to Charon, and he leered. "And enjoying the scenery."

The expression sent a chill up Charon's spine, and he shoved his hands into his pockets. The pair were standing near the door that led to the hallway, and he toyed with the idea of exiting through the kitchen and dining hall.

Rigel grinned broadly as he puffed up his chest. "Yep, I do consider myself pretty good-looking," he claimed, and Charon wondered if he blatantly misunderstood the man on purpose. Rigel held out his hand and stated, "I'm Enforcer Rigel, and you are?"

"Otzel," the dark-haired man replied, but he ignored Rigel's hand. Instead, he returned his creepy gaze to Charon. "And I was talking about the cute twink over there."

An annoyed rumble echoed through Charon's mind, and he knew if he hadn't been be-spelled, his dragon eyes would be flashing.

"Yeah, my man Charon is a pretty nice thing to look at," Rigel stated, returning his hand to his side. He strode toward Charon, ignoring that Otzel followed, holding Charon's gaze with his own dark eyes. Charon barely managed to keep still when Rigel slung his arm around his shoulders and tucked him close while saying, "Always makes me glad to know him." After flashing a reassuring smile at Charon, Rigel returned his attention to Otzel. "So, was there somewhere you needed help finding, Otzel?"

Otzel's nearly black eyes narrowed as he glanced between them. For just an instant, Charon felt certain he saw a flash of a vertical pupil in the guy's eyes. Then it was gone, and Otzel curved his lips into another creepy smile.

"No, I've seen everything I needed and found everything I wanted," Otzel claimed, shoving his hands into the pockets of his jeans. His voice full of innuendo, he stated, "I look forward to getting to know Charon, too."

After sweeping his gaze over Charon once more, Otzel turned and exited the room.

Charon felt a shiver rush through him, and he desperately wanted to change into his true form so he could fly away and hide. He finally understood the expression, undressing him with his eyes. Charon didn't need his dragon instincts to know that man was bad news with a capital B.

"Well, damn," Rigel muttered, squeezing Charon's shoulder lightly. "That guy's an asshole." After shaking his head, he focused on Charon, frowning with concern. "I don't know what kind of shifter he is, a reptile of some kind probably, but he's not one of the good ones. I'd recommend steering clear of him."

As Charon nodded, he wondered if he'd seen what he'd thought he'd seen and that Otzel really was a dragon. He stifled a hysterical laugh as he wondered how a dragon would feel to being pegged as a reptile. They were warm-blooded, after all, not that the average paranormal knew that. Considering dragons' reclusive natures, just like Rigel, few could recognize them by scent.

"I swung by hoping to catch you after your shift in the hopes of asking you on a date," Rigel admitted. With a wince, he added, "But now I feel like if I do ask and you agree, it'll be out of gratitude." Rigel grinned wryly. "So I'll ask you another time."

Charon managed a weak chuckle at the shifter's antics. "Um, thanks."

"But I will insist on walking you to your car," Rigel continued, easing his arm away so he could lower his hand to Charon's lower back. "Just in case that prick is hanging around."

Allowing Rigel to guide him forward, Charon murmured, "Thanks. Um, again." He hesitated a second before admitting, "And yeah. He totally gave me the creeps, too."

Rigel opened the door, and Charon half expected to see Otzel lurking just on the other side. Fortunately, the hallway was empty. Charon could only make out a faint musky smell he didn't recognize, and he wished he still had his heightened senses, which would have allowed him to confirm if Otzel truly was a dragon.

"Are you going to the barbeque at Dane's tomorrow?" Rigel asked, and Charon felt him tease his thumb over his spine.

The move sent a zing of . . . not arousal, but awareness . . . through Charon, and it took him a few seconds to find his tongue.

"Um, yeah," Charon confirmed. Racking his brain for more, he blurted out, "Dakota always says I don't have to bring anything, but I feel bad eating his and his brothers' food without contributing anything."

Rigel chuckled. "It's just their way." After opening the door to the parking garage, he stepped through first and glanced around quickly. Then Rigel asked, "Can I pick you up? That way you don't have to worry about driving." With a wink, he claimed, "I'd be happy to be your DD."

Charon opened his mouth, then closed it again. "Um." He paused, trying to remember when someone had offered a kindness without expecting anything in return. While Charon was aware that Rigel would be happy to take him up on a roll in the sack, he knew the shifter wouldn't push him for more than he was willing to give. Stopping beside the driver's door of his *Jeep*, Charon turned to Rigel, seeing the hopeful, expectant expression on his deeply tanned features. An odd thought struck him, and he blurted, "Do you think I'm your mate?"

Rigel's dark brows shot up his forehead. An instant later, they lowered as a sad smile curved his full lips. "Charon, you know about paranormals, so I would have told you immediately if that were the case." Rigel shrugged as he let out a sigh. Roving his attention over Charon's form, he stated, "And I would have been damn proud to have you as my mate." Lifting one large hand, Rigel crooked a forefinger and skimmed it along Charon's jaw. "I'm attracted to you. I won't lie. But you're not my mate."

An odd mixture of relief and disappointment swirled through Charon's gut.

Probably for the best. My life is a little messy right now.

Lifting a hand, Charon gently gripped Rigel's and eased it from his face. "Then I'd be happy to accept your offer of DD, but we're going just as friends."

Rigel nodded as he pretended to stab himself through the heart. "Story of my life." Then he winked and waggled his eyebrows. "But that doesn't mean I don't want you to think about all the fun we could still have."

Charon laughed at Rigel's silliness even as he rolled his eyes.

Then Rigel sobered, and he added, "As long as we both remember we're just having fun, and our life situations could change at any time, give it some thought."

Knowing what Rigel was saying—*my mate could come along at any time, and then our time together would come to a screeching halt*—Charon patted Rigel's chest.

"And that's exactly why I think it would be better if we stay friends."

Rigel heaved a clearly fake, put-upon sigh. "Gotta be the

voice of reason." Then he opened Charon's door while saying, "All right, all right." Taking a step back, Rigel ordered, "Text me your address. I'll pick you up at six."

Pleased at Rigel's understanding—and that he'd officially made a new friend—Charon pulled out his phone and did just that.

CHAPTER FIVE

"Charon came with Rigel?"

Dakota could barely get the question past the hard lump in his dry throat. A surge of jealous rage rushed through him, and he finally understood the expression, seeing red. He wanted to hunt the other enforcer down and throttle him.

Even his Komodo dragon perked up in his mind, rumbling questioningly.

Clenching and releasing his hands, Dakota breathed roughly through his nose. He closed his eyes and tipped his head back, struggling to get himself under control. His teeth ached as he clenched his jaw, grinding his teeth.

"Calm down, Dakota," Dane ordered.

Dakota was trying. Really, he was. He couldn't even begin to understand his reaction. Over the last couple of weeks, Dakota had done his best to keep his thoughts of Charon regulated strictly to the friend zone.

It hadn't always worked, and while Dakota wouldn't admit it to his brothers, he'd rubbed one out to thoughts of the small man on several occasions.

Feeling Dane wrap his arms around his shoulders, Dakota remained tense and still in his brother's hold.

"Danny, go get Del," Dane ordered softly, still holding Dakota in a tight embrace.

"I'm so sorry," Danny murmured, his voice growing quieter as the sound of his footsteps told Dakota that he was hurrying away. Dakota just heard Danny add, "I didn't realize Dakota had a thing for Charon."

"Is that true, Dakota?" Dane demanded quietly. "Do you have a thing for Charon?"

Dakota wasn't going to lie. After this reaction, there was no point in denying it anymore.

"Yeah," Dakota muttered. "I do."

"You do what?" Del asked, revealing his presence. "What the hell is going on?" Then he cursed softly, and Dakota felt his eldest brother's arms wrap around him from the other side as he asked again, "What happened?"

Filling his lungs with the scents of his brothers, Dakota finally felt his anger ease to a low simmer. He managed to unclench his hands, but he couldn't get more words past his throat. Fortunately, Dane answered Del.

"Danny walked in and made a comment about how Charon just arrived with Rigel." Dane began rubbing his hand up and down Dakota's spine, as if he worried that saying the words would set him off again. "My mate didn't know that Dakota has a crush on him."

"A crush," Dakota finally managed to grumble. "Makes it sound like I'm a damn teenager."

"Well, what would you call it?" Del moved a hand to the back of Dakota's neck and massaged lightly. Lowering his voice, he whispered roughly, "You said your dragon doesn't recognize Charon as your mate, so if it's not a crush, are you telling us that you've gone and fallen in love with someone other than your mate?"

Dakota's gut clenched upon hearing Del's blunt words.

"Did I really do that?" Dakota whispered. "Love?" The confusion and worry he felt replaced the rage, allowing him to calm down. Snapping open his eyelids, Dakota glanced between his brothers. Both men sported concerned expressions, and the scent of their worry mixed with his own. "How the hell could that happen? I barely know the man."

Dane blew out a quiet breath while Del pinched his lips together. His brothers exchanged a look. Del opened his mouth, then snapped it shut again.

Shaking his head, Dane just shrugged.

Swallowing hard, Dakota frowned.

Danny piped up, "You know, maybe if you get to know him better, you'll realize you don't actually like him after all." Dane released Dakota in favor of tugging his mate into his arms, and Danny snuggled against him as he continued, "Humans fall in and out of love all the time. Or maybe it's just infatuation."

"Danny has a point," Del agreed, keeping his hand on Dakota's neck as he lowered his other arm. "You've been practically stalking Charon for weeks before you even started this whole friendship campaign. Maybe you're not in love with him, but you definitely have an unhealthy obsession with him." Del frowned at him. "Now, you know my philosophy on fucking co-workers, but maybe you should. Get it out of your system. Whatever sparked your interest may ease after that."

Dakota grimaced upon hearing Del's crass suggestion, but he couldn't help but feel a surge of arousal, too.

"Yeah, Dakota wants him," Dane drawled, humor lacing his tone. "If you'd met him in a club, you'd have already —"

Lifting a hand, Dakota pointed his finger at Dane while snapping, "Don't finish that. Don't you dare."

Dane lifted one hand in placation, a smirk toying at the corners of his lips.

"Well, now that we've got that decided, you better head out there and woo Charon away from Rigel." Del patted Dakota on the back, adding, "Take him a glass of wine and see how he's doing. I left Miggs manning the grill, so I better get out there."

Dakota nodded as he began following his brother.

Dane remained in the kitchen, patting Dakota on the back as he passed him and Danny. "Good luck, Dakota. I'll be out in a few minutes."

After nodding again—he figured Dane intended to reassure Danny that he hadn't done anything wrong, which he hadn't—Dakota followed Del out of the house. As soon as the sliding door shut behind him, he headed to the drinks table. Dakota quickly poured a glass of white wine before grabbing a beer for himself.

Holding one in each hand, Dakota panned his attention over the area. He saw his friends relaxing in clusters of threes, fours, and fives, chatting and appearing to have a good time. To the left, near the deeper tree line, Dakota spotted Rigel talking with Desmond and Lyra, but Charon wasn't with them.

Dakota glanced around once more, and when he didn't see Charon, he figured asking Rigel would be his best bet. Stepping off the back deck, he strode toward the other shifter. Weaving between groups, Dakota greeted his friends as he passed them.

When Dakota reached Rigel's trio, he forced a smile and dipped his chin in greeting. "Hey, guys." Glancing at Lyra, he smirked and added, "Lyra."

Lyra, a beautiful brown-haired tiger shifter and a badass enforcer in her own right, grinned and waggled her eyebrows at him. "Dakota." Her attention landed on the white wine. "That for me, handsome?"

"Uh," Dakota responded, ever-so-eloquently, as Lyra began reaching for it. "I was actually looking for Charon." Still, he handed it over to her. "It's one I picked up because he mentioned it was a favorite, so I wanted to make certain he got some." With a shrug and a grin, Dakota added, "I'll get him another." Then he turned his attention to Rigel. "Heard Charon came with you, so I thought you might know where he is."

Rigel glanced behind him toward the trees while rubbing the back of his neck. "Charon said he needed some air and decided to go for a walk."

"Needed air?" Lyra snickered as she waved her hand. "We're in the woods."

"He looked a little jittery. Like he had too much caffeine or sugar before coming here," Desmond added, his brows drawing together in clear worry. "I offered to go with him, but he wanted to go alone."

Nodding, Rigel added, "I noticed a slight sheen of sweat, too." Rubbing his hand over his jaw, he stated thoughtfully, "I noticed an odd scent clinging to him, too. I hope he's not coming down with something."

The more the pair spoke, the more worried Dakota became. "I'll grab a bottle of water and go after him," he decided.

Rigel held up his hand. "But Charon said he wanted to be alone."

Dakota shook his head, already turning away from the group. "I don't want him to get lost, or if he's ill, I don't want him to fall or pass out or something."

Could dragons get sick?

"If he's fine, I'll leave him alone," Dakota continued. "Which way did he head?"

When the pair of men hesitated, Dakota clenched his free hand, trying to hide his impatience.

Finally, Desmond pointed north. "He headed through those trees around five minutes ago."

"Thanks." Then Dakota jogged back to the deck. He placed his beer next to Del's near the grill, who arched his brow in question. As Dakota grabbed a bottle of water, he told him, "Charon took a walk in the woods. Said he was feeling odd or something. I'm going to go find him. Make sure he's okay."

"Rigel let a human wander into the woods at night?" Del scowled in the other shifter's direction. "Did he even have a flashlight?"

"Uh, no idea," Dakota admitted, starting away from the deck once more.

Could dragons, even in human form, see as well as a shifter in the dark?

Dakota had so many questions for Charon.

"Hey, Dakota."

Pausing, Dakota turned back to face Del. His brother held out his hand as if to shake. Confused, Dakota went with it, and Del slipped something discreetly into his palm. When Dakota looked, he realized it was a single-use packet of lube.

Del shrugged. "I always carry a couple on me anymore."

Dakota nodded once, fighting the smirk that was trying to curve his lips. "Thanks." Then he hurried away.

Dakota made his way in the direction Desmond had indicated. After he was far enough away from the barbeque, he inhaled deeply, searching for Charon's scent. He weaved back and forth, trying to find the man's trail.

Finally, Dakota caught a whiff of Charon. As Rigel had mentioned, there was something else mixed in with it, too. To Dakota, it almost seemed as if Charon had recently been in close contact with another. The earthy scent caused Dakota's gut to warm for a new reason—arousal.

Ooooookaaaaay.

While Dakota wished he could hurry, due to the darkness, he ended up slowing. He used his sense of smell to keep himself on Charon's trail. Dakota found himself impressed by how far Charon had actually managed to travel.

To Dakota's confusion, the farther he walked, the more the unfamiliar scent took over, and the fainter the smell he associated with Charon became. He tried to pick up his pace, worried that someone was following Charon. No matter how pleasant the stranger's smell, Dakota refused to have him hurt the dishwasher he'd become infatuated with.

Not on my watch. Plus, the guy is on my property.

Dakota knew the signs. He'd left Dane's territory a moment before. Knowing their properties like the back of his hand, Dakota knew a clearing was just ahead, and he hoped he could catch both men there.

Except, when Dakota arrived at the clearing, there was no one there. Instead, in the middle of the small space, stood a dragon. The moonlight reflected off its light-purple scales, making them gleam metallically. It had its long, sinewy neck arched, and the wings were bent, resting the middle of the top boney ridge on the ground in lieu of forelegs.

"Holy shit," Dakota whispered, realizing he was finally seeing Charon in his true form. "You're magnificent."

His words must have been loud enough for Charon to hear, for the dragon peered toward him, his surprise clear, even on his dragon face.

Dakota began to lift his hands in placation, struggling with what else to say. Except, then the wind picked up, blowing Charon's dragon scent toward Dakota more strongly. The aroma of the stranger intensified, and his Komodo roared to life in his mind.

Mine!

Finally, it registered.

Charon smelled differently in his dragon form.

And this must be his true scent . . . and he really is my mate.

As Dakota processed the implications—why he'd become so infatuated with Charon becoming clear—for the first time in over a century, he lost control of his Komodo. His shift tore through his body, clothes falling away from his rapidly expanding form. Even as the human side of his brain stalled from shock, his animal side didn't hesitate an instant, and he began galloping toward his dragon mate.

Dakota was halfway to his mate when the way the dragon backed away from him registered with his human mind. Reining in his Komodo's exuberance, he slowed. He rumbled questioningly upon seeing an expression on the male's face that could only be trepidation.

How can a dragon look uneasy?

And why? He's my mate.

Except, why didn't Charon say anything?

Concern easing his excitement, Dakota growled softly as he continued to slowly approach the dragon. Instead of greeting him, the gorgeous dragon bowed his magnificent head. A second later, he began to shift.

As Charon's dragon frame shrank and the scales melted away, the heady scent of his mate's goodness decreased just as quickly. The smell Dakota associated with Charon returned. It once again began to mask the fact that the dragon was his mate, and Dakota's Komodo growled with annoyance, expressing his displeasure.

"I'm so sorry," Charon cried, staying on his knees with his arms wrapped around him. "It's the first time I've been able to completely take my true form, and I couldn't resist." Peering at Dakota through his lashes, Charon murmured, "Please forgive me for not asking permission to change in your territory. I—" Then his eyes widened, and a look of horror crossed his features. "Oh, gods. You're not even surprised to see a dragon here. Is this why you pushed to be my friend? You knew the spells were weakening." Charon began rocking slightly as he bowed his head. "You're going to tell Elder Gaithnos, aren't you? He sent you, didn't he? I don't want to be trapped again. I—"

Dakota stopped listening to Charon's mutterings, their words having lost their meaning somewhere along the way. With his heart aching for the young man falling apart before him, he shifted once more. Returning to human form took just as little time—only a handful of seconds—as it had taken to transition into his Komodo.

Immediately wrapping his arms around Charon, Dakota tugged the tense man toward him. He rocked back onto his ass, pulling his mate onto his lap. Nuzzling his lips against the smaller male's temple, Dakota did his best to soothe his clearly traumatized mate.

"It's okay, Charon," Dakota murmured, rubbing one hand up and down the man's back. Even as he relished the opportunity to touch his mate's smooth skin, he did his best to ignore his body's predictable response. "You are always welcome here, my mate. I would never stop you from taking your true form." Scoffing softly, Dakota added, "Hell, your dragon is magnificent. I hope you'll allow me the opportunity to explore you."

After a few moments, the man in Dakota's arms finally stopped trembling.

Dakota continued to rub his back and side with one hand and massage his neck with his other. Nuzzling Charon's temple with his own, he pressed his nose to the soft flesh behind his mate's ear. While Charon's human scent dominated, undertones of his mate's true dragon aroma lingered there, soothing Dakota's Komodo.

"D-Did you just call m-me your m-mate?"

Lifting his head upon hearing Charon's stuttered, clearly shocked words, Dakota met the man's questioning gaze.

"Yes," Dakota confirmed. "You are my mate."

"Really?" Charon squeaked, gaping at him.

Dakota nodded slowly. "Really." Frowning, he felt confusion of his own. "Can't you tell?"

Charon slowly shook his head as he nibbled his bottom lip. *Well, fuck.*

Tension flooding him, Dakota blurted, "Why the hell not?"

CHAPTER SIX

*W*hy the hell not, indeed.

    Charon stared into Dakota's intense green eyes. The man appeared clearly frustrated . . . and maybe a little offended. He didn't want that, and he racked his brain for a suitable answer.

Wait. Of course. That asshole!

"I smell completely human to you and everyone else, right?"

Dakota nodded once. "Except, now that I'm holding you." He tucked his nose behind Charon's ear, continuing to clutch him as he breathed against the sensitive skin there. "Here. I can make out your true scent right here." With a deep, satisfied-sounding sigh, Dakota murmured, "Delicious."

The hairs on Charon's neck stood on end when Dakota's warm breath ghosted across his skin. His blood heated in his veins. The warmth of Dakota's body pressing against his own finally registered, spreading erotic tingles everywhere they touched . . . which was a lot.

"D-Did you know I was a dragon before you started talking to me?" Charon couldn't resist asking the question. Dakota hadn't seemed surprised, after all.

"Mmm-hmmm," Dakota confirmed, continuing his erotic onslaught on Charon's skin, making it extremely difficult for him to think.

Still, Charon knew they needed to have a conversation. "H-How?"

"Mycroft told me," Dakota revealed, rubbing his hand up

and down Charon's side, almost distracting him. "Must have gotten distracted by his mate, and he let it slip." His warm breath continued to tease Charon's senses as he whispered, "Swore me to secrecy. Why?"

"That was another condition placed upon me. As few people as possible were to know I was a dragon," Charon told him, recalling how alone it had made him feel. "I-I didn't volunteer for my job as dragon liaison." Swallowing hard, he admitted, "This was a punishment."

That seemed to register with Dakota, for he lifted his head and met his gaze. "Why?" Frowning, he added, "A punishment from who?"

"An asshole named Elder Gaithnos." Charon couldn't help the growl that filled his tone. "I refused his son's suit to form a mate-bond. No way did I want his jerk of a son touching me, let alone have to carry his offspring."

A shudder went through Charon just at the idea of submitting to that dragon.

Dakota growled, the sound rumbling through him and vibrating against Charon due to the way he clutched him. "Well, you're mine," he snarled. He even glanced around as if he would find someone there to deny his claim. "They can both just fuck right off." Dakota's expression turned hungry as he swept a feral gaze over him. "I've waited for my mate for one hundred seventy-five years, Charon, and now that I've found you, I don't plan to wait. I intend to claim you and bond us this night."

The way Dakota's attention lingered over Charon's groin reminded Charon that he was naked. Feeling the shifter's erection pressing blatantly against his ass cheeks and lower back gave testament that he wasn't the only one. Even with his human senses, Charon could smell the arousal pouring off of Dakota, and it enflamed his own, making him shudder with desire.

As Dakota roved his hands over Charon's body, he rumbled gruffly, "Please tell me you don't have a problem with that, baby."

Charon felt on fire everywhere Dakota touched. His skin goose bumped, and the hairs on his arms and legs stood on end. Tingles skittered across his nerve endings. Gasping softly, he felt sweat bead on his flesh as his arousal surged.

Pushing into Dakota's touch, Charon began to writhe on the bigger man's lap. He didn't know if it was because it had been so long since he'd been touched that everything felt amplified or if it was because they were mates. Charon just knew he wanted more of it.

"Tell me yes, Charon," Dakota insisted, licking and nipping that spot he seemed to love behind Charon's ear. "I want you desperately, but I won't take you if you're not ready."

"I've wanted you for ages, Dakota," Charon admitted. Gripping the shifter's upper arms, he squeezed lightly to get his attention. When Dakota lifted his head, allowing Charon to peer into his lust-dilated eyes, he told him, "I would have let you fuck me even if we weren't mates." A niggle of doubt wormed its way into his gut, and Charon blurted, "We *are* mates, right? You're not lying about that?"

Dakota sobered as he shook his head. "I'm not lying about us being mates," he assured, sliding his hand up from Charon's neck to thread it into his hair. "When I found out you came to the barbeque with Rigel, I nearly lost it with jealousy. My brothers had to talk me down." Dakota rumbled huskily, "Even before this amazing discovery that you're my mate, I still wanted you and wanted you badly."

"You never seemed like it." Charon furrowed his brows as he took in Dakota's intense expression. "You always acted like you just wanted to be friends."

Grimacing, Dakota explained, "My brother, Del, he has a policy of don't shit where you work." With a roll of his deep green eyes, he added, "Essentially, don't fuck around with co-workers, or things could get awkward later. We've seen it happen time and time again when someone can't keep it in their pants." Dakota pinned his hungry gaze upon him again. "But after seeing how I responded when you came with Rigel, even they were encouraging me to pursue you."

"Really?" Charon didn't know how he felt about that, so he decided to think about it another time. "Um, okay." Peering into Dakota's eyes, Charon asked, "Where do we go from here?"

Dakota's full lips turned up into a hungry grin. "Well, first, I'm going to kiss you." With a wink, he began lowering his head as he continued, "After that, my mate, I'm going to open up your sexy ass and claim you."

Without waiting for a response, Dakota pressed his lips to Charon's. He trembled as he felt the other man's warm appendage slide along his bottom lip. Opening, Charon welcomed his new—and forever—lover's tongue into his mouth.

When Dakota's flavor burst across his taste buds, Charon groaned as he savored the shifter's deliciousness. His dragon grumbled within him as the knowledge that he was tasting his mate swept through his mind. As a human, Charon couldn't seem to scent Dakota as his one and only, but by tasting him, Charon knew.

This man is my mate. He's it for me.

Tangling his tongue with Dakota's, Charon gave as good as he got. He teased along his mate's appendage before suckling lightly. Charon pushed his own tongue into Dakota's mouth, taking a deeper taste of the other man, moaning roughly, gripping Dakota's shoulders tighter as he continued to eat hungrily at him.

Charon's body went up in flames. His blood pounded through his veins, and his erection flexed and pulsed. He felt his chute muscles clench and relax repeatedly as his body readied for coupling with his mate.

By the time Dakota broke the kiss, Charon's lungs were screaming for oxygen. He panted harshly, struggling to catch his breath. To Charon's pleasure, Dakota appeared in the same state, his chest heaving.

Charon lifted his hand and reverently teased his fingertips along Dakota's kiss-swollen lips. "It's you," he whispered, beyond ecstatic at Fate's gift. "My mate."

Dakota's eyes gleamed with his pleasure. "It's me," he agreed, his voice husky and deep. "You recognize me now?" he asked before nipping at the tip of Charon's finger.

Nodding, Charon felt his gut clench as his aching dick twitched with anticipation. "Yeah. Your taste," he admitted. "My dragon could taste you."

Chuckling, Dakota murmured, "Wish I'd given in to my desire and kissed you sooner."

Charon snickered before sobering. "But would you have believed me?"

"Yes," Dakota stated in a certain tone. "Absolutely. Everything I've been feeling these last few weeks finally makes sense." Tightening his arms, Dakota rocked to his feet, taking Charon with him, holding him in his arms. A grin split his lips as he started heading toward the edge of the clearing. "And now that I understand, I can't wait to have you."

Charon wrapped his arms around Dakota's shoulders and his legs around his waist. Clinging to him, he asked, "Are you taking me to your place?"

"Later," Dakota declared. "I can't wait that long."

Confused, Charon cocked his head. "Then what—"

"Lube in my jeans," Dakota told him. Snorting, he added, "Well, what's left of them."

Charon saw the pile of ruined fabric and recalled Dakota shifting right out of his clothes. "Can't believe you did that."

Dakota shrugged, not seeming upset in the least. "I finally caught your true scent. It shocked the hell out of me and fried my brain." Easing to his knees, Dakota gently placed Charon on the shreds of his clothes. He smiled at him, wonder in his expression as he stroked his fingertips along Charon's jaw. "Best fucking moment of my life, and it's just getting better."

Upon hearing Dakota's heartfelt words, Charon felt as if his heart fluttered in his chest. He opened his mouth, then closed it again. Uncertain what to say, he watched Dakota tug a single-use packet of lube from the pocket of his ruined jeans.

Seeing the slick, Charon realized they still had a few things to talk about. "Um, you won't need that."

Dakota tore open the packet before focusing on Charon. "I know some guys like the burn of being taken dry, but I'm a pretty big guy." He glanced toward his groin pointedly, where his probably ten-inch dick jutted from within a nest of close-cropped curls. Meeting Charon's gaze again, Dakota stated solemnly, "If that's a kink of yours, we'll do it on occasion, but not this first time. I'm not going to hurt you."

Warmed by Dakota's concern, Charon smiled up at him. "That's actually not a kink of mine," he admitted. "I was referring to the fact that . . . I'm an omega dragon."

With the way Dakota's brows furrowed, his confusion was easy to read. "What's that mean?"

"I'll explain about different dragon quirks later," Charon assured, not wanting to get into a lengthy explanation right then. His body was way too primed for sex, and he needed his shifter. Still, Charon quickly explained, "Suffice it to say, in the presence of their fated mate, an omega dragon's body responds to their arousal." Charon never thought he would have to explain omega dragon anatomy to anyone, and he suddenly found himself fighting a wash of embarrassment. Gamely, he finished, "I make my own slick, and my body loosens in preparation of being taken by my mate."

"Omega dragon," Dakota repeated quietly even as he slathered the lube on his fingers and dick. After tossing the empty packet to the grass, he levered over Charon, easing between his legs. "That's the sexiest fucking thing I've ever heard." Holding Charon's gaze, Dakota eased his fingers between his ass cheeks, feeling for his hole. His voice lowered to a husky rumble as he told him, "I can't wait to hear all about dragons and your culture. You become more fascinating with every new bit of information I learn about you." Dakota eased a finger into him, obviously testing his body's readiness. A wide smile creased the big man's lips before quickly slipping away. "You scent human. Are you human right now? And if so, how does your body know to prep itself?"

"Um, yeah, I'm human. I was be-spelled to be one while here on assignment." Charon nibbled his bottom lip, realizing their conversation had gotten derailed somewhere, and there was still so much to talk about. "I can feel it happening, so . . . maybe from your taste?" Gripping Dakota's shoulders, Charon whispered, "Maybe we should talk some more, because there's still so much I need to tell you."

"Nothing's more important than bonding your life thread with mine," Dakota declared, although he did pause in his ministrations of teasing Charon's hole. His expression turned pained. "Unless you've changed your mind."

Charon quickly shook his head. "Never. I want you so damn badly," he assured his shifter. "But I'm being punished, remember? Bonding with me could put you in danger."

A growl rumbled from Dakota, and he began moving his hand again. "That just means bonding is that much more important." Lowering his head, he pressed a slow, sipping kiss to Charon's lips. In between light pecks, Dakota whispered, "I know this is probably the most unromantic claiming in history, but we've been dancing around each other for weeks. I promise I'll make it up to you, baby."

Deciding to trust Dakota knew his own mind, Charon slid

his hands up his shifter's neck and threaded his fingers through his thick, dirty-blond hair. "You don't have to make up anything." Lifting his legs, he wrapped them around Dakota's waist. "However I can get you is perfect."

Groaning, Dakota sealed his mouth over Charon's, thrusting his tongue in deep.

Charon welcomed the invasion, reveling in the taking and the feel of Dakota's tongue rubbing again his own, over and over. Coupled with the fingers in his ass, teasing repeatedly over his prostate, Charon was pushed closer and closer to the edge so very swiftly.

With his dick aching and twitching, Charon turned his head and broke the kiss. "Now, Dakota," he pleaded, moving his hands to his shifter's shoulders and digging in his fingers. "Please now, my mate."

"Love how my name sounds on your lips, Charon," Dakota declared gruffly as he eased his fingers from Charon's hole. He lifted his head and pinned him with a feral grin. "And now."

Charon felt Dakota's cock head bump against his opening, and he tightened his legs, hoping to encourage him.

Dakota grinned broadly. "You're mine."

Then Dakota thrust, and Charon groaned as his prepared body relaxed and opened to his forever lover. As his shifter sank in and in, Charon felt stretched so perfectly. The sensation went straight to his head, and he moaned wantonly.

The glide across his prostate caused sparks to fire up his spine. His balls tightened. His cock throbbed. Feeling Dakota's chest slide across his own, even his nipples beaded.

To Charon's shock, his orgasm crashed over him, sending his senses soaring to the clouds. His dragon roared in his mind, and without a conscious thought, when Charon's teeth extended, he sank them deep into Dakota's shoulder.

Mine!

CHAPTER SEVEN

Dakota had barely bottomed out into the sweetest, tightest, hottest chute he'd ever experienced when pain pierced his shoulder. A second later, that morphed into tingles of fiery pleasure that rushed through his body with the speed of a freight train. With a gasp, he couldn't stop his balls from drawing up and his cock from erupting.

Barking Charon's name, Dakota rode on the waves of the headiest orgasm of his life. His eyes practically rolled back in his head as his body shook. His cock spurted burst after burst of seed deep inside his mate's willing body.

With spots dancing across his vision, Dakota barely registered it when Charon eased his teeth free. His Komodo did, however. He felt his teeth extend, and he allowed his instincts to take over.

Dakota lowered his head, licking a stripe along the sweet flesh where Charon's collarbone met his shoulder. A second later, he sank his teeth through that same skin. The flavor of Charon's blood flowed across Dakota's tongue, lighting up his taste buds with the exquisite ambrosia of his mate's life-giving fluid.

Sucking and licking, Dakota drank the sweet nectar as swiftly as he could pull it from Charon. He moaned against his flesh, reveling in the flavor. Dakota didn't think he would ever get enough of his dragon's taste, and he imagined himself turning into a vampire damn fast.

The moan and shudder of the man in his arms caught Dakota's attention just before the chute muscles wrapped around his erection squeezed and released. That, combined with the hot fluid heating his abdominals once more, told Dakota that his mate had come once more. His body responded by jerking his way through a second orgasm in a matter of seconds.

Pride filling him, Dakota carefully eased his teeth free of Charon's flesh. He lapped across his dragon's skin, cleaning the oozing blood away. The bite marks healed, leaving behind a gorgeous claiming scar, which Dakota couldn't resist taking a moment to kiss lightly.

Dakota lifted his head and peered at Charon. "Hello, my mate," he whispered, teasing the fingers of his hand through his dragon's blond hair.

To Dakota's surprise, Charon blushed as he peered at him through his lashes. "Hello, mate." He nibbled his bottom lip for a moment before adding, "I'm so sorry."

"For what?" Dakota asked, confusion filling him.

"For, um, coming so fast and biting you without permission." Charon blurted out the words so fast, Dakota barely understood them. His mate finished with, "I should have asked permission."

With a roll of his eyes, Dakota shook his head. "You're my mate, Charon. You can bite me any damn time you want. It felt fucking amazing." He waggled his brows as he added, "Plus, I'm damn proud to be wearing your mark."

Dakota didn't understand why Charon creased his brows or why he scented of surprise. Knowing they still had plenty to learn about each other, he figured he would discover it in time. To that end, and now that his raging hormones were satisfied—somewhat—Dakota decided a little more talking was in order.

Except, Dakota had no desire to separate from Charon. To that end, he murmured, "Hany on, baby." Then he eased one arm under Charon's torso and gripped his ass with the other as he rocked to the left. Hearing Charon's surprised squeak, Dakota rumbled, "Relax and move with me, my mate."

Once Dakota landed on his back, he helped Charon settle into a comfortable position on his chest. He rubbed up and down his dragon's back soothingly. At the same time, Dakota bent his legs so he could keep his half-hard dick encased within Charon's body.

Dakota threaded his fingers into Charon's hair once more, using the hold to get the man to tip his head. Once his mate had rested his chin on Dakota's chest, and their gazes met, he smiled widely. While massaging Charon's scalp, Dakota rubbed his still slightly slicked hand over the flesh of his back.

"So, why on earth would you think I wouldn't want you to mark me?" Dakota asked quietly.

"Um, because you're more dominant than me," Charon responded quietly. He swept his gaze over Dakota's face, so he just arched one brow, hoping for more information. Charon must have gotten the hint, for he added, "Only the dominant dragon marks their mate unless they discuss it ahead of time."

"Glad I'm a Komodo shifter and not a dragon," Dakota quipped with a wink. Grinning, he told his mate, "Anyway, don't worry about that. I love carrying your mark. In fact—"

Before Dakota could say more, the sound of a phone ringing filled the air. He groaned softly, recognizing the ringtone. Casting his hand to the left, Dakota felt around for the remnants of his jeans. When Charon shifted his weight as if to move off him, Dakota growled and tightened his other arm around his waist to keep him in place.

Charon snickered. "It'd be easier if I moved off of you."

"I like you right where you are," Dakota declared, casting a mock glare Charon's way. "It's perfect."

When Charon smirked and relaxed upon him again, Dakota returned to his hunt for his phone. By the time he'd tugged it free of the pocket, it had stopped ringing. He had just woken the device when it began to ring once more.

Dakota rolled his eyes as he accepted his brother's call. "What is so bloody important?"

"Did you find Charon?" Del asked without preamble, not bothering to comment on Dakota's annoyed tone.

"Yes," Dakota replied, unable to help but grin as he gazed upon Charon. "Charon is here with me. He's fine." With a cheeky wink, Dakota added, "Better than, actually."

"I take it you've officially stolen him from Rigel, then," Del commented dryly.

"Oh, yeah," Dakota replied as a fresh wave of jealousy ripped through him. He tightened his arm where it rested around Charon's waist. "Rigel isn't getting near my mate."

"I was never with Rigel," Charon murmured, frowning at Dakota. "We're just friends."

At the same time, Del asked slowly, "Your mate? I thought you said he wasn't your mate."

"I didn't think he was," Dakota admitted. With a heartfelt sigh, he stared into Charon's clear blue eyes. "But there's been a few developments that I'll need to share with you guys."

"I see." Del sounded concerned, but he didn't say more about that. Instead, he told him, "Rigel is talking about following you all out there. Guess he feels bad about letting Charon walk into the woods by himself." Before Dakota could respond, Del added, "Dane is trying to convince him to hang on a second, and I told him I'd call you. Why didn't you pick up right away?"

Dakota smirked as he replied, "Well, it took me a minute to reach my phone. I didn't want to move much because —"

Charon slapped his hand over Dakota's mouth, staring at him with wide eyes. Shaking his head quickly, he mouthed the word *no*.

Okay. My mate is a little shy. I'll have to remember that.

"Hmmm, I think I get the general idea," Del stated drolly. "I'll let Rigel know you're having some private time." After a second of hesitation, Del asked, "Are you coming back here tonight? Or should we bring you both breakfast at your place?"

Dakota held Charon's gaze as his lover eased his hand away from his mouth. "Breakfast at my place," he replied quietly. Then Dakota added, "But not too early."

Del snorted. "Right. See you at ten tomorrow."

"Something with bacon and sausage," Dakota requested cheekily.

"Of course."

Dakota could imagine Del rolling his eyes.

"Oh, and Dakota," Del continued, his voice lowering to a soothing rumble. "Congratulations, brother."

Grinning widely, Dakota replied, "Thanks, bro." A glance at his phone told him that Del had disconnected the line. After placing it on the grass, Dakota cocked his head as he eyed Charon. "So, Rigel giving you a ride to the barbeque wasn't a date thing?"

Charon shook his head. "No. How could I date him when the only one I was interested in was you?"

"Good answer," Dakota grumbled, feeling mollified by Charon's quick reassurance. Then he sobered, recalling their aborted conversation. "So, a dragon elder be-spelled you to be human because you wouldn't . . . wait a minute." Something Dakota's lust-addled brain hadn't picked up on before suddenly clicked. "Did you really say something about baring that asshole's young?"

Tensing in Dakota's hold, Charon stared at him with a deer in the headlights look. "Y-Yes," he whispered, a squeak even entering his voice.

Dakota realized a hint of gruffness had entered his tone. Even knowing it was due to shock, he felt bad that he'd sort of barked at his mate. Rubbing one hand up and down

Charon's back, he moved his other into his dragon's hair. Dakota used the hold to adjust Charon's position so he could tuck his nose against that sweet bit of skin behind his ear.

Breathing deeply several times, Dakota focused on getting his racing pulse under control.

Kids. Pregnancy. Holy shit!

Dakota had never considered kids before. He'd always been religious about using protection with women. With his mate being a man, it hadn't even occurred to him.

Is this what getting carried away because I was thinking with my dick could mean?

"I-If it m-makes you feel any better, I-I'm sure I c-can't get pregnant while be-spelled."

"Be-spelled." Dakota repeated the word on a whisper. He thought about what that meant. "You had a spell placed on you, making you appear and scent as human to the rest of us."

Charon nodded, and Dakota noticed the worry still lurking in his eyes. There was also the vestiges of fear in his scent.

Needing to banish that quick, fast, and in a hurry, Dakota whispered, "It's okay, baby." He pressed a quick kiss to the soft skin behind his mate's ear. "Even if I did knock you up, it wouldn't be entirely your fault."

Tipping his head a little, Charon peered at Dakota from beneath his lashes. "Sure it would be," he countered. "I'm the dragon, and you don't know anything about our kind. I'm the one who gave in to my omega urges before enlightening you of the consequences." As Charon's cheeks took on a deep pink hue, Charon muttered, "It's no wonder they ordered me be-spelled as a human. I can't control myself in the presence of deep arousal. I'm a dragon. I should be stronger than—"

Dakota pressed his palm to Charon's mouth, forcing him to stop speaking and ceasing his self-flagellation. "Oh, my mate," he murmured, shaking his head. "When I said I was partly responsible, I meant it." Dakota smirked as he shrugged one shoulder. "Hell, I'm the one who still has my dick in your ass."

Charon stiffened, his hands curling against Dakota's pectorals. His entire body felt tense as a bowstring. Even his channel clenched on Dakota's half-hard prick.

Fighting back a moan, knowing it wasn't appropriate under the circumstances, Dakota rubbed up and down Charon's back instead. He held his little mate's gaze steadily, letting him see that he wasn't upset.

Concerned, sure.

Worried, definitely.

Upset, not at all.

Dakota smiled as he lifted his head and pecked a kiss to Charon's lips. "So, you and I can father children together." He forced the words to come out even, calm. "That is truly . . . remarkable." Scoffing, Dakota murmured, "I thought that only gargoyles could knock up their male mates." After he pressed another kiss to Charon's lips, he softly stated, "I can't wait to hear about all our other differences."

After several long minutes, Charon remained quiet. While he continued to lie on top of Dakota's chest, he seemed almost frozen. His expression turned a little vacant, and his breaths came in swift, panting breaths.

Holding steady, Dakota did his best to soothe. He teased his fingertips through Charon's hair, massaging his scalp. His hand on his mate's back never stopped, petting the knobs of his spine and teasing the skin of his sides and ribs.

Finally, Charon began to relax once more. He blinked a few times, and he appeared to regain his focus. His brows furrowed just a little as he slowly unfurled his clenched hands and slid his palms over Dakota's chest.

"Y-You really believe that," Charon whispered. "Don't you?"

Dakota sighed deeply even as he continued his ministrations. "Baby," he purred, easing his hand out of Charon's hair so he could skim his fingertips along his dragon's full bottom lip. "Yes, I truly believe that. It takes two people to make a baby, and I'm one of us in this equation." As Dakota rocked his hips to accentuate his words, he added, "No matter what, we're in this together, baby." He furrowed his brows as his thoughts shunted through all their conversations, trying to piece together what he knew he was missing. Finally, it hit him. "And I'm not totally sure you're actually human, no matter what you smell like to us all."

"What do you mean?" Charon eased up on him a little, resting his chin on his palms where they were crossed over his chest. "Elder Gaithnos told me the spell turned me into a human and bound me so I couldn't access my true form."

"And, yet, neither of those things seem to be holding true, are they?" Dakota pressed. "Okay. Consider this." Unable to help himself, after all, Charon just felt too good, Dakota began rocking his hips slowly, easing his erection partway out, then back inside his mate. "I saw you return to your true form, so even be-spelled, it's possible."

Charon nibbled his bottom lip for a few seconds, his breath catching in his chest. He shivered a little before moaning. Then, with a groan, he began rolling his hips, moving in sync with Dakota's thrusts.

"I only just did that today," Charon admitted, his voice breathy and rough. "It's been almost ten years. Not since that damn spell."

Growling under his breath, Dakota muttered, "I seriously want to kick that elder's ass." Then he shook his head and added, "And now that I know what I'm looking for, I can discern a spot on you where your real scent emanates." With a feral rumble, Dakota added, "I just wouldn't want anyone else to tuck their nose against the side of your neck to experience it."

"W-Well, I have managed to gain some s-scales on my limbs in the last few weeks."

Dakota grinned broadly. "Hmmmm."

Shocks of pleasure trickled through Dakota's veins. The bliss of his cock easing in and out of Charon's hot, wet body was beginning to derail his thought chain. Knowing he needed to get it all out, Dakota slowed his ruts.

"Maybe that's because my scent has been affecting you," Dakota mused. "I've been around, watching you often." Scoffing, he smirked at his mate. "I've been a little stalkerish, actually."

Then Dakota sped up his hips once more.

Charon whimpered, telling Dakota that he'd found the perfect spot within his mate. "I-I-I—" He paused and groaned. Huffing a breath, Charon managed to ground out, "Just thought the old dragon who cast the spell was dying, so his spell was failing."

Humming, Dakota murmured, "I suppose that's a possibility, too." He couldn't resist speeding up his ruts. The feel of his mate's channel just felt too damn fantastic. Still, he managed to mumble, "But how do you account for your body readying itself for my cock if you're wholly human?"

Except, by that time, Charon seemed to have lost his tongue. He whined and rocked against Dakota, and Dakota was all for that.

We'll figure it all out later.

Shutting down his brain, Dakota gave in to his body's instinctual urges and spent the next hour of the warm spring evening coupling with his mate.

CHAPTER EIGHT

Charon decided he just might end up a morning person. Waking up with Dakota in his bed was going to make starting each day a joy. His mate's exuberance for putting their morning woods to good use was the stuff of legends.

Waking warm and snug, cradled in Dakota's arms, had felt amazing . . . until an experienced hand had wrapped around his half-hard dick. In just a few strokes, his shifter had brought him to hard and throbbing. His lover had then rolled them, lifting and maneuvering Charon, until Dakota lay on his back with Charon straddling his shoulders.

Dakota had swallowed his erection to the root, sucking strongly. He'd used one hand to fondle Charon's balls and his other played with his soon-to-be soaking chute. Hanging onto the headboard for dear life, it hadn't taken long for Charon to be howling Dakota's name as he spurted his seed down the shifter's throat.

After that, Dakota had eased him down his body so he straddled his groin. He'd sunk his erection deep within him, stretching him in the most perfect and primal of ways. As Charon had lain sprawled on Dakota's chest, his shifter had fucked his ass with long, languorous strokes until he'd come a second time before anointing his insides with his fluids.

"Good morning, my mate," Dakota had rumbled before taking Charon's mouth in a sensual kiss that threatened to start things all over again.

After that, Dakota had picked Charon up in his arms and

carried him to the shower, where he'd washed him thoroughly while whispering how he wanted to get him all dirty again.

Then . . . the nausea had hit.

Charon had choked back his urge to hurl as he'd rushed out of the shower. Making it to the toilet, he'd dropped to his knees. He'd emptied what little he had left in his stomach into the bowl.

Resting his head against his forearm, Charon tried to catch his breath. His stomach still swirled unpleasantly, and his body trembled from the aftershocks. He couldn't remember the last time he'd vomited.

Had the action always felt so violent and terrible . . . as if his body were betraying him?

Vaguely, Charon heard the shower water shut off. A few seconds later, he felt a towel being tucked around his body. Then a cool cloth was placed on the back of his neck.

Turning his head a little, Charon peered up at Dakota. He gave his lover a wan smile. "Thanks," he whispered, his voice slightly hoarse.

Dakota nodded, giving him an understanding smile. Kneeling beside him, he pressed a kiss to Charon's temple. "Be right back, my mate." Dakota rubbed his back gently before ordering, "Just rest here a moment."

Charon nodded again, not trusting himself to speak as his stomach began flipping some more.

His shifter had just exited the room when Charon had to lean over the bowl to throw up again.

Kneeling there, Charon gripped the towel around his shoulders with one hand. He allowed his mind to drift, his sole focus on taking one slow breath after another. His attention floated, and he found himself impressed with how clean the bathroom was.

Huh. Wonder if Dakota is just that neat or if he has a maid service.

Dakota returned, carrying a bottle of water and a steaming mug.

"Coffee?" Charon asked hopefully.

Smiling wryly, Dakota shook his head. "Afraid not." He set the mug on the counter. "It's tea. I didn't have any ginger tea, so I found some ground ginger in my spice rack." Easing to his knees beside Charon, Dakota popped open the bottle of water and offered it to him. "I don't know if it'll do as much good as real ginger tea, but hopefully, it'll help a little. I also texted Dane and asked him to run out and get some real ginger tea and bring it with breakfast."

"Ginger tea?" Charon took the water and sipped carefully. He swished it around his mouth before spitting it into the toilet. "Why ginger tea?"

Dakota's brows furrowed. "I thought that was what helped women when they're pregnant. Do dragons use something else for nausea?" Scoffing softly, he shook his head as he muttered, "At least we know fast, huh?" All the while he spoke, he gently rubbed a soothing hand over Charon's back.

Charon realized to what Dakota was referring. "Oh, shit," he hissed. Staring at his mate for several heartbeats, he felt his mind scrambling for another explanation. Except, there really wasn't. "You think I'm pregnant."

Even though Charon didn't phrase it as a question, Dakota still nodded.

"I-I'm so sorry," Charon whispered. He needed to blink quickly as the backs of his eyes suddenly burned. "I didn't . . . I mean . . . I—"

"Hey, *hey*," Dakota crooned. Wrapping his arms around Charon, he rocked back and tugged him onto his lap. "I'm not upset." Dakota nuzzled his lips against the sensitive skin behind Charon's ear as he whispered, "It takes two to make a baby, remember? I'm just as much at fault as you." Then Dakota lifted his head and grinned sheepishly. "I asked Dane to grab a pregnancy test, too. Talk about questions from him, but I told him I'd explain everything when they got here." With a wince, he added, "They might be early, so, um . . . if you're feeling up to standing and brushing your teeth, I'll get you some sweats and a shirt."

Charon realized then that Dakota already wore a pair of sweats, although he'd skipped a top, putting his gorgeous, thickly muscled torso on display. He could so easily become distracted by his mate's smooth, tanned skin. The tan of his areolas contrasted beautifully with his lighter nipples, begging to be sucked.

"Hey. Eyes up here, baby," Dakota teased, placing his forefinger under Charon's chin and encouraging him to meet his gaze. Seeing his shifter's twinkling green eyes, Charon fought back a blush, even as Dakota murmured, "I do love the way you look at me, Charon."

"You're gorgeous, Dakota," Charon stated with a shrug. "Surely plenty of people have told you that."

Dakota lifted one shoulder in his own half-shrug. "The only person's whose opinion counts is yours."

Charon sucked in a sharp breath upon hearing Dakota's words. It wasn't a declaration of love or anything, but it told him how much his shifter cared about him. His heart beat wildly as he nibbled his bottom lip, uncertain how to respond.

As if sensing his internal struggle, Dakota didn't wait for a response. "How are you feeling?" He jerked his chin in the direction of the tea. "It'll probably be best when it's hot."

"I can stand," Charon claimed. While he wouldn't call his stomach settled, he no longer felt the urge to hug the toilet.

Dakota nodded, taking him at his word. With ease that always impressed Charon, the big shifter lifted him and held him steady as he found his feet. He then rose gracefully before rummaging in a drawer and pulling out a new two-pack of toothbrushes. After opening one side and withdrawing a green-handled brush that boasted a rotating circular head, Dakota handed it to Charon.

Then Dakota removed the other new one — one with a blue handle — while admitting, "Just bought 'em. Was ready for a new one myself, and the two-pack was on sale."

"Thanks," Charon stated simply.

After wetting the brush, Charon accepted a dollop of toothpaste from the tube Dakota held. Standing before the sink, he brushed his teeth. Charon found brushing his teeth with another, even if he was standing at the next sink over, to be an oddly intimate act.

Once Charon had finished, he set his toothbrush in the brass mug at the side of the sink next to Dakota's.

"Try the tea," Dakota encouraged before pecking a kiss to Charon's lips. "I'll grab you some clothes and let you finish up in here."

Charon smiled and nodded. Even though he wasn't much for tea, he still did as Dakota had bidden. After all, his mate had gone to the trouble of making it.

After taking a sip, Charon analyzed the taste. It seemed that Dakota had used a kind of mint tea for the base, which was pleasant. Charon didn't know how much ginger the shifter had added to it, but he could only catch a hint of the flavor.

He'd just taken another, larger sip when his bladder made itself known. After setting down the mug, he closed the door and returned to the toilet. Once he'd done his business, he washed up, wrapped the towel around his waist, and headed out of the room.

Clothes had been set out on the bed, and Charon quickly donned them. The sweatpants fit well, as did the long-sleeved top. A niggle of jealousy slithered through Charon as he wondered whose clothes they were.

Charon exited the bedroom, his mug of tea in hand. Hearing voices, he paused, hesitating. The deep tones of Dakota's brother Del reached him, but he couldn't quite make out the words.

After a deep gulp of tea and a few deep breaths, Charon felt ready for what he knew would be an inquisition.

Exiting the hallway, Charon saw Miggs spreading a plethora of Styrofoam *to go* boxes out on the table. He either heard or scented him, for the little guinea pig shifter immediately turned toward him. Miggs grinned widely and straightened.

"Morning," Miggs greeted perkily. Then he sobered. "I'm sorry to hear you're not feeling the greatest." A smile once again began toying around the corners of his lips. "So, you're really a shifter who can carry young. What kind? Why did you hide it?" Miggs frowned. "I suppose it's only been in the last few years that the Shifter Council has started making some radical changes."

Charon finally managed to get a word in and admitted, "I didn't hide on purpose." With a shrug, he waved a hand toward himself. "This was done to me. Not my choice."

"Who did it to you?" Del asked coldly, sauntering into the room. "Why?"

The steaming mug he carried smelled of coffee, and Charon found his mouth watering. Then he focused on Del's question. "Um, Elder Gaithnos."

"Never heard of him," Del stated, pinning him with a narrow-eyed stare. "What's he an elder of?"

"This isn't an interrogation, Del," Dakota reminded, frowning at his brother. He slung an arm around Charon's waist and began guiding him toward the front room. "Let's eat in the living room. It'll be more comfortable for my mate."

Scoffing, Charon forced his feet to stop, making Dakota do the same. "I'm one day pregnant," he stated with a laugh. "I think I can handle sitting at the table." Easing away from Dakota, Charon gripped his hand and started leading him back that way. "Besides, Miggs already set everything up. Can I have a cup of coffee?" He held up his empty mug. "I finished my tea, and my stomach feels a lot better."

Even as Dakota allowed himself to be guided to the table, he stated, "I didn't think pregnant women were supposed to have coffee. At least, not much of it."

Charon shook his head, deciding to go with amused rather than annoyed. "Well, that's human *women*." Squeezing Dakota's hand, he pointed out, "As we've discovered by now, I may smell totally human to you guys, but internally, I'm obviously not." Charon waved toward his still flat belly. "I'm a dragon. Remember? We can have coffee."

"Holy shit," Dane whispered from behind them, announcing that he'd arrived and let himself and Danny in. "Did you just say you're a dragon?"

"Yep." Dakota grinned broadly as he tucked Charon against his side. "My mate is a fucking dragon. A real one."

Del snorted. "What's that supposed to mean? A *real* one."

Dane rolled his eyes. "He's making fun of the fact that we're called dragons, even though we don't have wings or scales."

"Or breathe fire," Dakota added with a grin.

Unable to help himself, Charon piped up, "Not all dragons breathe fire. Some of us breathe ice."

Dakota grinned broadly and squeezed him close. "See? Epic."

Shaking his head, Dane guided a still clearly shocked Danny into the room. As he helped his mate into a seat, he grumbled, "It's probably why Dakota rides that damn crotch rocket. He's compensating for his lack of wings."

"What?" Dakota asked hotly, although his outrage sounded feigned to Charon's ears. "I just feel the need for speed."

"I'd love to go for a ride on your motorcycle," Charon cut in. "It looks like fun."

He decided to refrain from admitting his thoughts from a few weeks before — that it would be the best he could get to flying without his true form.

"I'd be happy to take you out, baby," Dakota told him, an approving gleam lighting his green eyes. "I know you'll love it."

Charon grinned, pleased.

Dakota dipped his head and pecked a kiss to his lips. "Okay. Coffee. How do you take it?"

"Creamer, if you have it," Charon requested. "Otherwise, black."

"Not a fan of plain old milk?" Dane asked, settling beside Danny. Then he pointed at him. "Glad Danny's clothes fit you. We forgot to think about bringing something else."

With the answer to where the clothes came from easing Charon's mind, he settled into a chair to enjoy breakfast. Too bad the second they opened the container with the scrambled eggs and the scent hit his nose, he had to go running for the hall bathroom. Charon hit his knees in front of the toilet, spewing up his water and tea.

Dakota swiftly followed, a fresh mug of real ginger tea in hand . . . as well as the pregnancy test Dane had picked up, just to be sure.

Damn. So much for the coffee.

CHAPTER NINE

"I'm so sorry," Miggs said for what had to be the fifth time. The small shifter was sitting on Del's lap in the living room, while Del took up most of the small sofa. "I didn't even think—" Miggs wrung his hands as he shook his head.

"It's fine, Miggs. Really," Charon assured . . . again. He smiled wryly at Miggs. "It certainly never would have occurred to me that scrambled eggs would set off my nausea. I certainly wouldn't have." Charon scoffed as he added, "Normally, I love eggs."

Dakota rubbed up and down Charon's back, pleased his mate didn't mind when he'd pulled him onto his lap after settling in a large chair.

Dane and Danny were curled up together on a different love seat.

Once Miggs had taken the eggs outside—those who wanted some ate them while standing on the back deck—Dakota had guided a chagrined Charon back to the dining room. He'd been pleased when his mate had managed to eat half a dozen strips of bacon as well as several pieces of buttered toast. Dakota had been concerned he wouldn't be able to keep it down, but the ginger tea seemed to be doing the trick.

After that, Dakota had made Charon a fresh cup of coffee, and they'd all moved to the living room.

Dakota knew it was now question and answer time.

"So, this Elder Gaithnos is a dragon," Del mused, relaxing with his own coffee. "Why did he have a spell cast on you?"

Dakota listened as Charon explained about Elder Gaithnos's son, Glindber, who wanted his mate for his own. His Komodo's ire rose upon hearing that Gaithnos had manipulated the king into thinking Charon wanted the dragon liaison position. On top of that, the elder went so far as to get the king to agree to Charon being be-spelled so everyone thought he was human.

For his own good, the elder had insisted.

Plus, very few people were allowed to know the truth.

Mycroft must have been really distracted by finding his mate to have shared Charon's truth with me.

Dakota would never be more grateful, since the fact that Charon was a dragon was what had drawn his attention to the reclusive little man.

"Does Gaithnos still have King Leortis's ear?" Dane asked curiously, his brown eyes narrowed.

Dakota could practically see the wheels turning in his brother's head.

Charon shook his head. "I don't know," he admitted. "My contact is Salazar. I give him my reports about what's going on in the Shifter Council, and Salazar gives me the reports that King Leortis wants shared with the council."

"How do you know the reports are from King Leortis?" Del asked, always the suspicious one. "The ability to scent a lie has been stripped from you, hasn't it?"

Charon opened his mouth, then closed it again. "Um." He glanced toward Dakota, who squeezed his side, offering his mate silent reassurance. Returning his attention to Del, Charon shrugged. "I can't imagine anyone going behind King Leortis's back like that." Charon sounded scandalized. "That'd amount to treason and would carry a death sentence."

Growling, Del grumbled, "And yet, people looking for power do that kind of shit all the time." His hazel eyes narrowed as he mused, "So, our first order of business is to locate a warlock who can remove that spell on you."

Dakota appreciated that his brother took charge, since he knew his brain was still a little scrambled by the whole finding his mate and knocking him up activities. Still, he needed Charon safe above all else.

"Only if removing the spell won't hurt Charon," Dakota countered. After a second, he quickly added, "Or the baby."

Del arched one brow and stated, "That went without saying."

Dakota nodded. "Uh, right."

Of course. I should have known better than to think my brother would ever put my mate in jeopardy.

Gods, these new instincts are going to take some getting used to.

"I'll talk to Councilman Regales," Dane claimed. His brother was damn near the grizzly shifter's best friend outside of the councilman's human mate. Dane had been the one to convince Regales to attend their barbeques and holiday gatherings. "He should know about warlocks in the area, and he'll be discreet about it."

"And I'll make some inquiries about Salazar." Del began threading his fingers through Miggs's hair, seeming to soothe himself from whatever he was thinking. "If I find out he can't be trusted, we'll need another point of contact." After glancing at Dakota, Del focused on Charon. "Is there anyone you trust? Family? Best friend?"

Charon grimaced as he shook his head once. "No, I don't know who my parents were. Some dragons don't want to raise an omega, believing that males carrying young is unnatural." When Dakota couldn't hold back his growl, Charon smiled at him while rubbing his chest and saying, "At least, they took me to the king rather than selling me to one of the weirs that raise omegas to be sold or traded."

"There are groups of dragons out there that do that?" Danny whispered, his expression one of horror.

"Sadly, there are still human and other paranormal groups

that do that to others," Dane pointed out before pecking a kiss to Danny's temple. "As much as it sucks, there are always those who care for nothing but themselves and their own money, position, or power."

"That doesn't mean it's right," Danny grumbled.

"No, it doesn't," Dane agreed as Danny cuddled into his side.

"And friends?" Del pressed, returning them to the task at hand.

With a sigh, Charon admitted, "I only had a small circle of friends, and we weren't real close. After they heard about my new assignment here in Savannah, they wished me good luck before ending communication." Rubbing his free hand over his opposite arm—the one that held his cup of coffee—Charon muttered, "I know it's because they didn't want to get on the elder's bad side, either, but gods, that makes me sound like a loser."

"No, it makes them sound like assholes," Dakota declared, growling softly. "Well, now you have plenty of new friends and family." Curving his lips into a cheeky grin, he glanced between Dane and Del before adding, "Even if they are pains in the asses sometimes."

Before either of his brothers could quip back, Charon muttered, "Better to have well-meaning, supportive pains in the ass brothers than to have none at all."

"Well put," Dane jumped in, grinning broadly. He winked at Charon before focusing on Dakota. "Besides, it takes a village to raise a kid. Who else would you call on when you need a babysitter so you guys can have a date night?"

Dakota sobered as he thought of that. "Damn, my life is about to change."

Dane chortled for a few seconds until Danny elbowed him in the gut. "Hey, since you just volunteered us, *you* get to change the dirty diapers."

That shut Dane up damn fast, and he even gulped loudly as his face went a little pale.

"Well, you can call me anytime. I have loads of experience with babies," Miggs announced, bouncing a little with obvious excitement. "I'll help you set up the nursery and pick out clothes and make supply lists and" — his brown eyes lit up as he continued to tick things off on his fingers — "we'll need bottles and formula and . . . oh, do omega dragons produce their own milk?" Miggs leaned forward eagerly and asked, "How do you give birth? How long are you pregnant? Do you think it'll be a boy or a girl? Do you want one or the other? Ever thought about names? We could look online at name meanings and —"

Dakota felt his lips twitch upon hearing Miggs's excited words. He would have thought the cute guinea pig shifter had had too much coffee. Except, Dakota knew that Miggs didn't like coffee and didn't touch the stuff . . . unless it was off Del's lips, anyway.

Finally, Del slipped his hand over Miggs's mouth, ceasing his enthusiastic ramblings. When his mate looked up at him, his brown eyes wide and full of questions, Del rumbled, "I'm certain they'll appreciate all your help once the whole pregnancy thing settles in." His smile turning indulgent, Del added, "They're newly mated. We need to let them settle in a little first."

Miggs nodded behind Del's hand, and Del lowered his palm. Immediately, the guinea pig shifter refocused on them and stated, "You'll need help moving in here, Charon. Can't settle in if you're not together." Grinning, he asked, "Where do you live now? Do you rent or own? Link works in the tech center for the Shifter Council, and he has a brother named Bruins. Bruins is a realtor. He'll be able to sell your place for you."

"Uh, I rent a condo," Charon hurriedly cut in. "So no realtor needed." He peered shyly at Dakota. "We didn't really talk about moving in, yet. Is that—"

"Yes," Dakota declared, unwilling to allow his mate to have even a fraction of a second of doubt. "I want you here with me." Wrapping the fingers of one hand around Charon's nape, Dakota stated, "And Miggs did voice some valid concerns. How long *is* a dragon's pregnancy? A shifter's depends on the species involved. All the Komodo dragon shifter pregnancies in our bank were in the six months range, give or take a week."

Charon's brows furrowed. "Both male and female dragons lay an egg after four months. Parents are in their dragon forms at the time, and they use their elements to immediately hatch the egg."

Dakota thought he rattled off the information by rote, as if reading it out of a manual. "Uh, have you ever seen a dragon birth?"

Nibbling his bottom lip, Charon shook his head.

"What if both parents aren't present?" Dane asked, rubbing a hand over his jaw, and Dakota read the concern in his eyes. "Or if one of the parents isn't a dragon?"

"Uhhh . . ." Charon swallowed so hard his Adam's apple bobbed. "I-I suppose a family member would step in?"

"You don't sound completely certain," Del pointed out.

Scenting Charon's unease, Dakota pressed a kiss to the fragrant flesh behind his ear. "Don't worry," he whispered, doing his best to shelf his own nerves. "We'll figure this out. We have time."

Gods, between four and six months. In four to six months, I'll have a babe to take care of. Or dragonling.

"I figure if a dragon gets a human woman pregnant, then she'll have a human child," Dakota mused, thinking quickly. "Same if it's a shifter female. I wonder what happens if it's a dragon female and a shifter." When Dakota saw the others staring at him blankly, he finished his thought chain by say-ing, "Does the dragon genes always win out, or could the child end up being a shifter, instead?"

As Dakota finished his thought, he focused on Charon and arched a brow in silent question.

Charon shook his head as he blew out a breath. "Um, I can't remember any story where that's happened." Twisting his lips in a grimace, he admitted, "Dragons are sort of elitists. A lot of us can be real assholes." Charon's cheeks took on a pink-ish hue as he admitted, "I was for a long time. Why do you think I don't have shifter friends? I came to work, did my job, occasionally met with Mycroft or a councilman, and went home." The more Charon spoke, the darker his cheeks became as the scent of his embarrassment filled the room. Peering at Dakota through his lashes, he whispered, "It was meeting you, talking to you and your friends, that convinced me shift-ers weren't that way."

"What way?" Del pressed. Then he smirked and revealed his assholishness. "Unworthy of a dragon's time?"

Charon ducked his head, even as he nodded.

Del chuckled darkly. "Well, I've met plenty of shifters and humans who aren't worth the air they breathe, so I won't hold it against you." When Charon jerked his head up and stared at Del with wide eyes, Dakota's brother shrugged his wide shoulders. "You remember some of the dicks on the council and within the ranks of the enforcers before that shake-up a few years ago. Right?"

Nodding slowly, Charon slowly began to smile. "Good rid-dance."

"Exactly." Del grinned toothily. "So, we have a few months to do some research and reconnaissance on dragons." He nod-ded, obviously mentally processing something. "Plenty of time."

Dakota sure hoped so. Hugging his mate a little tighter, he

hoped his brothers couldn't scent his uncertainty. Within the space of twenty-four hours, Dakota had not only gained a mate to care for, but an unborn child.

He and his Komodo were on the same page. They didn't want to let Charon out of their sight. Unfortunately, with both their jobs, that just wasn't feasible.

"Hey, um, I-I don't know if this is bad form or something," Danny began, stumbling over his words here and there. "But, um, could I, uh, I mean . . . could you, well."

"Take a breath, my mate," Dane encouraged, rubbing his human's side. "Then just ask." With a warm smile, he stated, "We're all family here."

Danny nibbled his bottom lip for a few seconds, before blurting out, "Will you show us your dragon, please?"

Dakota grinned at Charon, curious as to see how his mate would respond. In truth, he would love to see his dragon's gorgeous form again, too. He had only enjoyed a fleeting opportunity the evening before.

"R-Really?" Charon sounded so very surprised by Danny's request.

To Dakota's pleasure, every other man in the room nodded—Miggs with a wide grin and enthusiasm. Dane smiled indulgently at Danny as he, too, nodded. Del gave a single reserved head-nod.

When Charon peered up at Dakota, he quickly nodded, too.

"I-I could try," Charon began, his brows furrowing. "Before last night, I couldn't transform completely. The spell wouldn't let me."

"You were gorgeous last night, baby," Dakota assured. "If you can manage it, I'd love to see your stunning purple scales in the sunlight." Then he sobered and added, "Only if it doesn't hurt the baby."

Charon scoffed as he rolled his eyes. "We give birth in our

dragon form." Smirking, he continued, "Why would it hurt us?"

"Okay, smartass," Dakota replied, enjoying Charon's show of spirit. His mate had always seemed so reserved, and he hoped this display would come out more and more. "Finish your coffee, and we'll head outside."

Charon grinned as he brought his mug to his lips. As he swallowed the last of the brew, he looked so damn happy with the drink. Once done, Charon lowered his mug and eased from Dakota's lap.

"That vanilla creamer you have is really good," Charon told him. "I'm surprised I've never tried it before."

"Glad you like it. It's one of my favorites." Dakota rose to his feet, too, noticing the others doing the same. Sliding his fingers into Charon's, he urged, "Come on. I can't wait to see you again."

"Will you shift for me, too?"

Surprised to hear the hesitancy in Charon's tone, Dakota released his hand to wrap his arm around his waist. "Of course. I know my Komodo would love to play with your dragon, too."

Charon grinned up at him. "Okay."

Dakota led the way outside. The warm spring mid-morning air caressed his skin, reminding him that he wore only a pair of sweats. It suddenly occurred to him that in a few seconds, his new mate would have to get naked.

"Turn around, everyone," Dakota barked when he saw Charon reaching for the hem of his shirt. Seeing Dane's smirk and Del's arched brow, Dakota quickly added, "Please. Newly mated and all."

Danny quickly spun, his cheeks turning a pinkish hue. The human had been a virgin when Dane had found him, and Dakota knew he was still getting used to a shifter's comfort with nudity . . . at least, most of the time. Call him possessive, but

Dakota wasn't ready to share Charon's gorgeous human form with anyone, yet.

"Here we go," Charon murmured, redrawing Dakota's attention.

Charon crouched on the grass with his head bowed. For several long moments, nothing happened. The lines of Charon's back seemed to tense and relax a few times, but that was it.

Dakota was about to tell Charon they could try another time, not wanting his dragon to feel pressured, when the most amazing thing happened.

Unlike when a shifter changed forms, there was no snapping of bones or crack of tendons. Charon's skin didn't ripple as his body took on a new shape.

Instead, between one second and the next, Charon's human form disappeared and a metallic-purple-scaled dragon towered over Dakota. His dragon's alluring scent flooded the clearing, and Dakota's Komodo rumbled approvingly. One thing Dakota knew for certain, the removal of the damn spell couldn't come soon enough.

"You are magnificent, Charon," Dakota stated, pleasure and awe filling him in equal measure.

To Dakota's delight, Charon lowered his cylindrical head and nuzzled Dakota's shoulder.

A second later, Dakota nearly lost his feet in shock when Charon rumbled, "Thank you, my mate."

CHAPTER TEN

As Charon unloaded a dishwasher in the Shifter Council Headquarters' kitchens, he let his mind drift. He couldn't believe how much of a difference a few days could make. So much had changed.

He'd spent several hours as a dragon. After Dakota's brothers and their mates had spent several minutes oohing and aahing over him—which had felt so very fantastic—they'd left with promises to meet him and Dakota at Charon's place Monday evening. Then, for the first time in nearly a decade, Charon had gotten to fly. He'd remained low, winging between treetops to avoid detection, while Dakota's Komodo galloped below him on the ground. They'd ended up in that clearing where he'd shifted the prior evening, and they'd made love and just held each other for a while.

When they'd returned to the house, Dakota had grilled steaks and baked potatoes. He'd opened a bottle of Charon's favorite white wine, and they'd curled up in front of the fire to share more stories about each other.

Of course, that was only after Charon had assured Dakota that alcohol wouldn't harm the growing egg within him. After all, dragon biology was vastly different to a human's.

As promised, on Monday evening, Dakota's family met them at Charon's place and helped him pack. The condo had come mostly furnished, so at least he didn't have to worry about what to do with all the stuff. Charon had given his notice to the condo manager, Amelia.

As it turned out, Amelia was a mink shifter. She'd been

shocked to find out that Charon was Dakota's mate, but she'd wished him well. Then she'd assured him that he would not be penalized for ending the lease early.

"Congratulations, guys." Amelia had grinned widely, looking so happy for them. Before she'd closed the door, she'd pinned a serious look on Dakota and ordered, "Treat him right, Enforcer Dakota."

Dakota had nodded seriously. "I will, Amelia. Make no mistake of that."

"You scent a little different today."

Charon nearly dropped the plate he'd been about to stack in the cupboard. Clutching it to his chest, he spun and frowned at Desmond.

"Damn it, Desmond," Charon snapped at the shifter who'd yanked him out of his pleasant memories. "Don't startle me like that."

Desmond lifted his hands in placation, although one held a hand towel in it. "Sorry, Charon." The fox shifter grinned as he lowered his hands, not appearing sorry at all. "I thought you heard me walk up behind you." Waggling his eyebrows, Desmond teased, "You must have been off in your own little world there, buddy."

"I was," Charon admitted, unable to help but smile as he recalled his thoughts.

Desmond whistled. "Damn. I know that look." Cocking his head in a very canine way, he asked, "Who's the lucky fella?"

"How do you know it's a he?" Charon asked curiously.

Tapping the side of his nose, Desmond told him, "Like I said. You smell a little different today." He leaned close and took a deeper whiff. "There's definitely a masculine scent clinging to you that wasn't there be—" Desmond reared back a step and gaped at him. His deep brown eyes widened. "Oh, shit," he whispered. "That's Dakota's scent on you. Are you—" He paused and shook his head before easing close to Charon once more. In a whisper, Desmond stated, "I know he went after you when you weren't feeling well at the barbeque, but that was days ago."

Desmond hadn't worked on Monday, Charon recalled, and now it was Wednesday.

"Um, well," Charon began, hesitating.

They hadn't discussed sharing their relationship with co-workers—outside of Mycroft, of course. Then Charon realized how ridiculous he was being. As soon as they broke the spell on him, there were going to be so many questions. Charon knew that Dakota would be beside him every step of the way.

"As it turns out, Dakota is my mate." Still, Charon kept his voice down. He didn't want his revelation to disrupt everyone working in the kitchen, after all.

Narrowing his eyes, Desmond gave him a searching look even as he shook his head once. "I don't understand," he admitted. "You guys have been in close proximity for weeks, and I kinda think Dakota is the sort of guy to jump in with both feet." Then Desmond scoffed and added, "Plus, he's hot and a genuinely nice guy. How the hell"—he paused and shook his head again—"*why* the hell would you resist him for so long?"

Letting out a deep sigh, Charon figured plenty of people would end up asking those same questions. "It's complicated," Charon decided to go with. When he saw Desmond's disbelieving look, he added, "And magick is involved." Waving toward his own chest, he explained, "It's a long story, but let's just say that this isn't what I smell like or what I really look like." Feeling a niggle of unease, Charon lowered his voice further and admitted, "I wasn't supposed to tell anyone, but Dakota found out, and he's my mate, and he and his brothers are helping me break the spell."

"Well, damn. That sucks." Desmond frowned as he patted

Charon on the shoulder. Offering him a wry smile, he added, "I'm happy for you. Damn jealous because Dakota is a catch, but happy for you." Taking a step backward, Desmond added, "And that definitely answers my question about your scent and why you were so far in your own head." He sobered once more, and before turning away from him, he offered, "If there's anything I can do to help, let me know. Okay?"

Charon smiled and nodded. "Thanks, Des."

As Desmond nodded and moved away, Charon returned to work, realizing he had a bigger support system than he'd even realized.

Nearing the end of his shift, Charon found himself filled with anticipation. He was no longer going home to an empty condo. Instead, he was heading to Dakota's home.

Now, my home.

Our home.

He would never get tired of those thoughts.

Charon glanced toward the clock, willing the hands to move faster.

Five minutes before the official end of his shift, Charon was putting the finishing touches on a set of pans that couldn't be run through the dishwasher. After so many years in the position, he'd become quite adept at timing everything pretty perfectly. Charon even appreciated the monotony of it as it left him with very few surprises.

With a dish towel in hand, Charon was drying the second to last pan when the door to his left opened — the one that led to the locker room. He noticed it in his peripheral but didn't think anything about it. There were always people coming and going for their shifts.

"Put the pan down, Charon," a deep voice ordered. "You're coming with me."

Snapping his attention up, Charon gaped upon seeing Otzel standing there leering at him.

"Yup, your mouth open and ready to offer service is a good look on you." Otzel gripped his package suggestively, and his eyes seemed to glow from within, telling Charon that Otzel's dragon was peering out at him. "If I get you to him quickly, he may even let me have a piece of you . . . as long as I wear a condom, of course."

Charon backed a step on instinct. "No," he whispered, gripping the pan as if it could save him.

"No?" Otzel growled the word. "I think you're confused." Lunging forward, Otzel used his long stride to easily close the distance between them, and he grabbed Charon by the upper arm. "Now, put the pan down. It's time to go." Then he snorted and rolled his eyes. "Or bring it with. I don't care. Maybe it'll be fun to paddle your ass with it."

"Hey, I don't know who you think you are," Chef Gage cut in, moving toward them. The black bear eyed Otzel with clear distaste in his whiskey-colored eyes. "But the man said no."

"That's right. You don't know who I am," Otzel countered, sneering as he swept his gaze over Gage's thickly built frame and slightly paunched belly. "Go back to your cookies, and stay out of what don't concern you."

Gage stood his ground, crossing his brawny arms over his chest. The bear shifter stood a good two inches shorter than Otzel's six-foot-four-inch height, but he still managed to appear to be looking down at him when he said, "My kitchen. My rules." Then he pointed toward the door. "Get out."

Scoffing, Otzel stated, "That's exactly what I'm doing." Then he began attempting to drag Charon toward the door.

Charon did his best to dig in his heels. Even though he had no idea what kind of dragon Otzel could be, he knew he was no match for him. He wouldn't have been even if he hadn't been be-spelled to be a human.

Out of the corner of his eye, Charon noticed Desmond nibbling his bottom lip as he checked his phone. A second later,

Gage grabbed Otzel's wrist. Whatever he did must have hurt, for Otzel released Charon.

Taking advantage, Charon scurried back a few steps, although he was loath to leave Gage to face Otzel's wrath. He knew the bear shifter was actually a very sweet and loving man. There was no way he could best a dragon, and Charon just bet that Otzel would be a guy who would fight dirty.

True to Charon's concern, Otzel feinted as if intending to grab for Charon again. When Gage pivoted in an obvious attempt to stop him, Otzel swung a big fist. He connected with Gage's jaw, sending the bear shifter flying backward into a counter.

Charon cringed when Gage tumbled to the floor, his head hitting the hard linoleum.

"You wanna get someone else hurt, Charon?" Otzel snarled as he cracked his knuckles. "Or you ready to come?"

Indecision flooded Charon. No, he didn't want to see anyone hurt. Except, there was also no way in hell he wanted to go anywhere with this dragon.

Otzel must have decided Charon's silence was a yes, for he reached for him again.

Acting on instinct, Charon swung the pan. He connected with Otzel's wrist, forcing his hand away from him. The back of the dragon's hand connected with the metal countertop, and he roared — probably in pain and anger.

Otzel lunged forward, swinging his other arm as he went.

Charon didn't move fast enough, and Otzel's backhand sent him sprawling to the floor.

An angry roar filled the kitchen, heralding Dakota as he rushed into the room. Seeing his mate's angry features sent a fissure of fear mixed with relief through Charon. Charon knew Dakota was a badass enforcer, but how could he prevail over a dragon?

Praying to whichever gods cared to listen for Dakota's

safety, Charon curled into a fetal position and watched the action play out.

Dakota grabbed Otzel from behind in a headlock. Even being a couple of inches shorter, he still managed to lift the larger man off his feet. Otzel crunched his abdominals, rested his booted feet against the counter's edge, and shoved. Both men went reeling backward.

When Dakota's ass hit the counter behind him, he lost his grip on Otzel. The dragon took advantage, leaping forward and pivoting. Otzel lifted both hands into fists in a defensive position as he swept his gaze over Dakota.

"Stand down." Del roared the order as he strode into the kitchen. "Both of you."

"He attacked me from behind," Otzel snarled. "I want him locked up."

Del narrowed his eyes, and he seemed to take in the scene in an instant. Justin knelt at Gage's side. The line cook was busy running his fingers through the bear shifter's hair, probably searching for injury. Desmond knelt beside Charon, rubbing his back, but Charon wasn't ready to move just yet as he waited to see what would happen.

"Enforcer Dakota is well within his right to protect those under his charge," Del stated calmly. "Not to mention, you hit his mate. Naughty, naughty. That's a punishable offense." Holding up his hand, palm up, he ordered, "Cuffs, please, Enforcer Dane."

"What the fuck are you talking about?" Otzel snapped. His eyes narrowed as he glanced toward Gage, obviously misunderstanding Del. "How the fuck was I to know that bear had a mate?" Curling his lip, Otzel added, "Besides. It was self-defense. He tried to stop me from taking Charon out of here."

Dane had plopped a set of cuffs into Del's hand, and the eldest brother began stalking toward Otzel. "And now you've just admitted to attempting to kidnap Enforcer Dakota's mate." With a cold look that Charon hoped never to have pinned on him, Del rumbled, "You really need to get your facts straight before entering Shifter Headquarters and trying to remove someone against their will. Trying to take a shifter's mate is also a punishable offense."

Otzel's eyes narrowed, and his nostrils flared. Then he lifted his chin and stated, "I'm a dragon. So is Charon." With a haughty expression, Otzel declared, "Your shifter laws do not apply to us."

Del gripped Otzel's shoulder and spun him, tugging one arm behind his back. After slapping the cuffs on his wrists, Del leaned forward and hissed into Otzel's ear, "We shall see . . . *dragon*." Then Del began pushing him toward the rear exit, calling over his shoulder, "Dane, Dakota, I want a report as soon as possible."

Before the door closed behind them, Otzel called, "I'll be out of here within the hour, Charon. See you again soon." Then on a cold laugh, he hollered, "Glindber is looking forward to seeing you, too."

Just as Charon was certain Otzel had intended, the dragon's words sent a chill of fear through his veins. He trembled where he still lay on the floor. When Dakota lifted Charon into his arms, Charon clung to his mate.

"He's come for me," Charon whispered, meeting Dakota's worried green eyes. "What am I going to do?"

Dakota growled softly as he pinned Charon with a hard look. "We're going to be just fine, my mate."

CHAPTER ELEVEN

"What the hell do you mean we couldn't hold him?" Dakota roared, anger surging through him. "That asshole knocked out one of our chefs and was trying to kidnap my mate." Pointing his finger at Mycroft, Dakota added, "His words."

"I'm sorry, Dakota," Mycroft stated, shaking his head. "Otzel is a dragon, not a shifter. Their laws are slightly different than ours." A pained expression crossed his freckled features even as he ran his hand through his red hair. "I didn't have a choice in this."

"There's always a choice," Dakota snarled, thrusting his hand through his own hair, mimicking Mycroft's move in agitation. "You could have told them Otzel was killed during the scuffle. I would have been happy to make it so."

"Dakota," Mycroft growled softly in warning.

Except, Dakota really didn't care that he was mouthing off to his boss—friend or not. Mycroft had let Otzel go free. Letting out a low growl, Dakota tried to decide how he could fix the problem.

I'll track him down. There must be a way to track a dragon. I'll—

Del gripped Dakota's neck in a loose hold. "Try to calm yourself, Dakota," he urged, using his thumb to massage the base of his skull. "Your mate needs you here, now, more than ever," Del rumbled into his ear, as if he knew exactly what Dakota was contemplating. "Don't lose your head over this."

Dakota glared at Del. "When a rogue shifter came into that very kitchen and tried to kidnap your mate, what did you do?"

Sighing deeply, Del smiled tightly. "I kicked the ass of anyone who tried to get in my way, and the rogues were caught and executed."

"Exactly," Dakota grumbled. Waving a hand toward Mycroft, he continued to scowl at his brother. "They weren't let go, giving them the opportunity to try again."

"Otzel wasn't just let go, Dakota," Mycroft assured, lifting his hands in placation. "He was remanded into the custody of a dragon elder and a dragon enforcer. I've also lodged a complaint with the king, warning him that our laws need to be respected by his people. Either that, or we get to treat his people by our laws."

Dakota took one breath, then two, as he tried to calm down. That had to be something at least . . . right?

"Where is Charon now?" Mycroft asked softly. "Is he okay?"

"He's in our quarters resting, right now. Miggs, Danny, and Dane are with them." There was no way Dakota would have been able to leave Charon alone, even to go to a mandatory summons from his boss. "Doctor Bulgazi checked Charon over after he was done with Gage." He rubbed a palm over his face, adding absently, "Both he and the baby are fine."

Dakota made a mental note to thank the bear shifter. If Gage hadn't intervened, ending up with a head injury, Dakota wasn't certain he would have arrived in time to stop Otzel from taking Charon. He also realized he needed to thank Desmond. The fox shifter had been the one to send him a 9-1-1 message. Dakota didn't think he'd ever sprinted through the corridors faster.

"I'm sorry. What did you just say?"

"Hmm?" Dakota lifted his head, confused to see the incredulous expression on Mycroft's face. "What?"

"You just shocked the shit out of our boss," Del stated dryly. "You mentioned the baby."

Dakota winced. "Yeah. Um, about that." With a shrug of one shoulder, he met Mycroft's gaze. "Charon is an omega dragon. I'm pretty sure I knocked him up that first time when we bonded." Dakota forced a wry smile he didn't truly feel. "In about four to six months, I'm going to need to take some paternity leave. Plus, I'm going to try to get Charon to quit the dishwashing job." He scrubbed a hand through his hair, massaging his scalp as he absently finished, "It's totally up to him if he wants to keep being the dragon liaison."

"Well, holy shit," Mycroft whispered, scoffing. Then he smiled widely. "Congratulations. When you told me Charon was your mate and you hadn't realized it because of the spell on him, I was happy for you both. Now." Barking a laugh, Mycroft grinned at him. "This is the first babe born to anyone working on the shifter council in . . . decades."

In hindsight, Dakota thought that those in charge should have taken that as a sign from Fate . . . a sign that they were doing something wrong.

Still, it's fixed now. Or being fixed.

"What about Councilman Shane Alvaro's daughter?" Del pointed out. "She's only a couple of years old now."

Mycroft waved his hand as if shooing away a fly. "Naw, doesn't count. Shane had the babe before he became a councilman," Mycroft pointed out. He rounded his desk and headed toward the sideboard. "This calls for a celebratory drink."

While Dakota would rather have returned to Charon and cuddled up in bed with him, he followed Mycroft to the other side of his office. Hell, maybe he needed a few minutes to decide how to break this disastrous news to Charon. He and his Komodo still railed against the fact that Otzel had been given to someone else's custody.

Bastards.

Dakota accepted the tumbler, his nose telling him it was a pretty high-end whiskey.

"To your future babe, Dakota." Mycroft lifted his tumbler.

Del and Dakota followed his lead.

"May his or her future be bright and trouble-free," Mycroft continued, grinning as he began bringing his tumbler to his lips.

Holding up his hand, Del stayed Mycroft's movements. "Not completely trouble-free," he countered, frowning. "One must experience some adversity. Otherwise, how will they ever grow as a person?"

Mycroft smirked as he rolled his eyes. "Okay." Holding up his glass again, he stated solemnly, "May his or her future be bright and full of adversity that will help him or her grow into the amazing person they will surely become."

Del nodded, obviously much happier with that toast. "To Dakota's kid," he stated, lifting his glass. Smiling warmly at Dakota, he offered, "Congratulations, brother."

"Thanks." Lifting his glass, Dakota murmured, "To my kid's future."

The three men clinked their glasses, then drank.

Dakota sipped once, pleased at the fine whiskey's flavor. Tipping it back again, he filled his mouth with a larger swallow.

"So, who came to get Otzel?" Del asked. "I want to check into him or her."

Just as Dakota swallowed, Mycroft replied, "Elder Gaithnos and his son, Enforcer Glindber."

Choking on his drink, Dakota sputtered, nearly spraying it across the room. He barely managed to get it down, Del patting his back as he snarled, "What did you say? Enforcer who?"

Mycroft glanced between them with his brows furrowed as he repeated, "Elder Gaithnos and his son, Enforcer Glindber."

"Yeah, that's what I thought you said," Del snarled before stalking back toward the desk. "Shit. Where's the hard copy of my report?"

After another concerned glance at Dakota, Mycroft followed Del. "In here."

Dakota's eyes were watering as he coughed through several breaths. His hands trembled, so he set the nearly empty tumbler on the sideboard. Then Dakota followed his brother and Mycroft in time to see his boss open a hidden door and step into a large room full of filing cabinets. He pulled a file from a locked drawer before returning to them.

Huh. Who knew his boss was partial to paper.

"Not a word of that room," Mycroft ordered, handing the file to Del. His green eyes narrowed in warning. "After realizing how corrupted our data systems ended up, I started keeping hard copies of certain files . . . just in case."

Del nodded absently as he was busy flipping through the pages. With a growl, he held the open file toward Mycroft and pointed to a paragraph. "On the way out of the room, Otzel made a comment, taunting Charon, yelled it really, about Glindber looking forward to seeing him again." Mycroft began to pale even as Del flipped through another couple of pages until he paused and pointed at another statement. "This is Charon's account, to the best of his ability while traumatized. Dane reported that Otzel said he was taking him to someone, and maybe he could have Charon's ass as long as he wore a rubber."

"Also," Dakota began, having to pause a second to clear his throat. "Charon told us that Elder Gaithnos was the one that tricked the king into assigning Charon into this position with so many safeguards, all because Charon didn't want to enter a mate-bond with Gaithnos's son, Glindber." He lifted his fingers and made air quotes. "Magick spells and shit, but the king didn't overview the process. He trusted Gaithnos to do it. Did you know that the fucking elder trapped Charon as a human until just a few days ago? We think the spells were weakening because I was around more, and I'm his mate, even though neither one of us knew it at the time."

"Oh gods," Mycroft mumbled, leaning heavily against his desk. "I really hate the picture you're painting for me." Scrubbing his hand over his face, Mycroft whispered, "But he's already mated and pregnant, so what's the point of coming after him now?"

Del tossed the file onto Mycroft's desk before crossing his arms over his chest. "Obsessed people don't really need a motive. That's why it's called an obsession." He shrugged his broad shoulders. "But in this case, I bet someone here was keeping tabs on Charon, and they noticed him spending time with us rather than just being a good little recluse."

"It was no longer a punishment," Dakota mused. "He was making friends."

"Exactly." Del growled under his breath. "And because of my big mouth, they know that Charon is mated to you. Shit."

Heaving a sigh, Dakota touched Del's upper arm. "You didn't know it would turn out like this."

Del didn't appear mollified. "Just like Mycroft didn't know any of this." Frowning, he stared at the floor. "We need another conversation about everything with Charon." Pinning Dakota with a hard stare, his brother asked, "Do you think Charon will be up for that?"

Dakota nodded. "Yeah. My mate is strong," he declared. "He'll be able to handle it."

"Good." Del touched the hard copy of the report. "Out of curiosity, does this hard copy match what's online?"

Instead of answering, Mycroft settled in his chair and woke his machine. He entered a password, opened a program, then entered another password. With a few more taps, he had the report open and was scrolling through it.

Pausing at Del's account, Mycroft cursed under his breath.

He quickly went to Dane's retelling of Charon's statement and muttered another explicative.

That told Dakota all he needed to know.

"We have a problem in the IT department," Mycroft snarled, grabbing his phone. Then he paused, his hand hovering over the device. "If I call down there, it's going to tip our hand."

"Occasionally, Link goes to our barbeques," Dakota mused, thinking of the large, bald musk ox shifter. "He was at the first one Charon ever went to several weeks ago."

"No way is Link the problem," Mycroft stated, shaking his head. "He's as loyal to us as they come. I'd trust that shifter with my life." Glancing between them, Mycroft added, "Same as I would with you guys."

Dakota felt his gut warm upon hearing Mycroft's praise, even under the shitty circumstances. "Thanks, boss-man," he teased, forcing a bit of joviality into his voice.

"I'd trust Link, too," Del commented, rubbing his chin. Narrowing his eyes, he mused, "But he may have made a comment about Charon being there while at work. We need to talk to him."

"We should make certain he's at our next barbeque," Dakota stated. Then he scowled. "But that's in four days."

Del peered Dakota's way, his expression going hard. "I have an idea, but you're not going to like it."

Growling under his breath, Dakota could guess at where his brother's brain had gone. "No way are we using Charon as bait."

"Hear me out," Del countered, lifting his hands, palms out. "Never once would he be left alone, and we'll have our trusted friends and family with us at all times."

Dakota stared hard at Del for a long moment. He knew his brother would never purposefully put Charon in harm's way. The bond between them all was just too tight.

That means I need to trust him.

Except, Dakota realized just that fast that it wasn't his decision alone. "We'll have to run whatever by Charon first," he stated. "I won't do anything he doesn't agree to."

Del's lips curved into a wide smile. "Well, hell," he rumbled, pleasure filling his tone. "My baby bro's finally figured out how to be in a relationship."

Groaning, Dakota grumbled, "Shut up," as he punched Del in the upper arm. Of course, then he had to shake out his hand because the big asshole had flexed his bicep, making it damn hurt. "Jerk."

Tipping his head back, Del laughed loudly. Then he patted Dakota on the shoulder and started toward the door. "Come on, man." Pausing, he turned and peered over his shoulder at Mycroft. "I'm hoping you'll come, sir."

Mycroft nodded. "Right behind you." Then he picked up the file and returned it to the secret storage room.

Even as Dakota prayed Del's idea wasn't what he thought it would be, he knew his brother well enough to know better.

Dakota's Komodo rumbled irritably in the back of his mind, and he breathed deeply, trying to keep his trepidation in check.

This is going to suck.

Chapter Twelve

Charon relaxed in Dakota's arms, deliciously sated. His body hummed from the sensual onslaught his mate had bestowed upon him for the last hour. Dakota had massaged, stroked, kissed, and nipped just about every inch of his body.

Even though Charon knew part of it was done out of fear, he'd still enjoyed every second of it.

But now, it's time to get this show on the road.

Charon also knew that Dakota was damn worried about what would most likely happen over the next couple of hours. In truth, he was, too. Except, he felt a certain amount of anticipation, too.

Perhaps, just perhaps, this can all come to an end.

Then my new life can begin.

With that thought in mind, Charon lifted his head and pressed a kiss to the underside of Dakota's chin. "We'd better get up, or we won't have time for a shower."

Dakota tipped his chin down and met his gaze.

The expression on his shifter's face nearly took Charon's breath away. There was no other way to describe it. The glow of love filled his deep green eyes as he smiled at him.

"I rather like the idea of my scent saturating every inch of you right now," Dakota admitted softly. As he threaded his fingers through Charon's hair in the way he absolutely loved, his Komodo asked, "Would it be so bad if every paranormal there could scent we'd just been intimate?" Dakota waggled his brows playfully. "We are newly mated, after all."

Unable to deny his mate anything, Charon grinned. "If

that's what you want, my shifter." Then he pecked Dakota's lips with a light kiss.

When Charon began to pull away, Dakota tightened his hold on his hair, keeping him in place. He eased his tongue into Charon's mouth, conquering him in a slow assault. He mapped every inch of Charon's cavity anew, as if exploring for the first time.

Charon teased his tongue against Dakota's, enjoying the sensuality. When his dick began to stir, he groaned and turned his head. Even the tug to his scalp when he pulled away didn't dull the heat beginning to thrum through him.

"You're so bad," Charon grumbled. "Now I'm going to be half-hard when the first guests arrive."

"But you love that about me anyway," Dakota declared with a grin, his tone light and teasing.

Taking the chance, Charon nodded as he held Dakota's gaze. "Yes, I do love you, Dakota."

Dakota's smile turned nearly blinding. "As I love you, my dragon." Then he leaned forward and pressed his lips to Charon's in a hard kiss. When he broke away, his green eyes glittered with intensity. "Love you, Charon."

Charon smiled back. "Love you, too, my Komodo."

Laughing, Dakota sat up and swung his legs to the floor. "Come on. Let's get dressed." As he headed to the dresser and began pulling out jeans, he sobered and added, "The sooner we get this over with, the sooner we can put these assholes behind us."

"I'll second that."

Charon caught the jeans Dakota tossed to him and began to dress.

Just as Charon feared, he sported a semi when the first people began to arrive, which happened to be Dane and Danny. While Dane smirked, he didn't say anything. Being human,

Danny remained pretty oblivious — *thank the gods.*

Del and Miggs arrived right after them, and Del wasn't nearly as circumspect. Arching one brow, he stated drolly, "You could have just pissed a circle around him, Dakota." Miggs smacked Del on the stomach, causing Del to chuckle and say, "Well, he could have."

When Danny glanced up at Dane, clearly confused, his lover leaned down and explained, causing Danny's face to take on a pinkish hue.

The guy really is cute.

Before much more could be said, several more cars appeared from between the trees shielding the driveway from the road. The six of them stood on the front deck, watching as a number of people poured from them. Finally, nerves caused Charon's arousal to flee.

Charon recognized Desmond and Link from two of the cars. Councilman Regales and his human mate, Theo, exited another. From Rigel's truck, he was joined by Lyra. From the passenger side of Mycroft's vehicle climbed a wiry blond man that he recalled was Boyd — Mycroft's vampire mate. The man that exited a pale blue sedan flagged Charon's attention — a slender, dark-featured, black male with gray just teasing at his temples and around the edges of his goatee. The man's black-eyed gaze roved over the group, lingering the longest on Charon.

"Most of you know where the barbeque is," Dakota called, waving while pointing off to the side. "Head on back while Mycroft introduces us to our new friend."

Once hellos and congratulations were hollered, along with a few lewd comments, the others disappeared from view.

Mycroft beckoned to the black man, and they climbed onto the deck. "Dakota, Charon. Good to see you both," Mycroft said by way of greeting. Then he smirked and added, "Smell you both."

Boyd chuckled as he nodded. "Not a bad smell, though,"

he quipped with a wink. "Good to see you both again." With a rakish grin that showed off his fangs, he told them, "I'll let you guys get to business and meet you out back."

Then Boyd dipped his head and pecked a kiss to Mycroft's lips before heading around back with the others.

Indicating the dark-featured male, Mycroft stated, "This is Urskin Claspin, and he's a warlock." His expression turned grim as he added, "I've explained the situation, and I'm hoping he can help."

"We're hopeful you can, too," Dakota declared, holding out his hand to the man. "Thank you for coming."

Urskin reached out and shook Dakota's hand with a nod. "It has been a long time since shifters have contacted me about working magick on a paranormal." He turned his attention on Charon, and as they shook hands, he narrowed his eyes. Slowly, Urskin shook his head. "You, however, are not a shifter."

Charon pulled his hand away, and Urskin didn't try to keep it. Instead, the warlock focused on Mycroft. "I cannot perform magick on a dragon. Even one that appears human."

"Damn," Dane muttered. "How the hell can you tell? Even our noses couldn't discern it."

Focusing on Dane, Urskin explained, "I see the auras of paranormals." He pointed at Charon. "His does not match." Chuckling softly, Urskin admitted, "Although it has been a very long time since I've come into contact with one of his kind."

"We know you can't cast a spell on a dragon," Mycroft cut in. Before Urskin could question him further, he continued, "But could you remove a spell that has been placed on one?"

"*Remove* a spell?" Urskin returned his attention to Charon.

While the warlock appeared to look at him, it felt more as if he were looking *through* him, leaving Charon slightly unsettled. He eased closer to Dakota, who instantly put his arm around him.

The move seemed to draw Urskin out of . . . whatever it was . . . for he smiled at Charon before turning back to Mycroft. "That is a fascinating proposition." Again, he turned back to Charon. "With your permission, I would be happy to try." Lifting his hands, Urskin quickly added, "Please know, I will do nothing that could harm you or your unborn babe."

"Damn," Danny whispered, glancing up at Dane. "He knows about that, too!"

Urskin smiled at Danny. "I am an old warlock, young one." His expression turning rueful, he shrugged. "I've had the time to learn how to pick up on many things."

Even as Danny began to blush, Dane dipped his head and pecked a kiss to his cheek.

"Let's head around back, then," Dakota urged, indicating where the others had headed. "We'll get comfortable, and you can let us know what you think you'll need."

After Urskin nodded his acceptance, Dakota moved his hand to the small of Charon's back, which he secretly loved, and began guiding him forward. Charon still remembered the first time he'd crossed these planks. He'd been so nervous, so worried, but everyone had made him feel so welcomed.

Charon would always remember that day as a new beginning.

"How long have you been cursed, Charon?" Urskin asked conversationally. "I can see that the edges of it have begun to fray."

"Uh, nearly ten years," Charon admitted. As he saw Urskin nod, a thoughtful expression in his deep dark eyes, he went on to share, "I pissed off an elder dragon because I refused his son's suit."

Scoffing, Urskin mused, "Dragons can be prideful beasts." Then, as if remembering who he was talking to, he quickly added, "No offense."

Charon snorted. "Uh, none taken. I had some pride issues of my own to deal with." Rolling his eyes, he added, "Still dealing with."

Dakota shrugged. "We all have issues of some kind." Having reached the backyard, he asked, "Can I get you a drink, Urskin? We have a hell of an assortment."

"Water for now, please," Urskin replied as he crossed to a table and pulled off the small messenger bag he carried. As he placed it on the table, he smiled slightly at Dakota. "A beer later, perhaps. It's been a hell of a long time since I've been to a barbeque."

"Sounds good," Dakota agreed. He glanced toward Dane, and Charon noticed that the brother headed to the beverage table with Danny at his side. Dakota returned his attention to Urskin, who was busy pulling out small pouches. "Do you need anything?"

"I was going to ask for a quiet place to work," Urskin admitted before glancing around, his gaze falling on the piles of folded clothes near the clearings' edge. "But it seems everyone has gone for a run."

Del hummed. "Working up an appetite. I'll start the grill." As he moved away, he asked, "You like burgers, hot dogs, brats?"

"All of the above." Urskin turned his attention to Mycroft. "They don't intend to attack me the second I start working on Charon. Do they?"

Scoffing, Mycroft shook his head. "No. We're hoping they'll be celebrating the lifting of the curse with us." He shrugged, adding, "On my word, you are safe from us."

Urskin dipped his head, taking him at face value. Then he focused on Charon. "Please remove your shirt and lie on the chaise lounge, face down." He pointed to a large lounger. After Charon lay down, Urskin rested his palm on his shoulder — not the one with his mating mark. "Try to relax, Charon.

My hope is that this will not hurt in the slightest." Then he hummed. "You may perhaps feel a tickling sensation across your flesh."

After crossing back to the table, picking up something, and returning, Urskin rested it on Charon's back. "This is an incense cone. The smoke will enhance the view of your aura to me," he explained as he used a match to light it on fire. "This will make it easier for me to see what spell has been done to you." With another reassuring squeeze to Charon's shoulder, Urskin offered, "Dakota can sit and hold your hand, if you wish. It will not jeopardize the spell."

Charon couldn't help his embarrassed smile. "I thought I was hiding it pretty well."

Urskin smiled kindly at him in an almost fatherly way. "I see your aura, Charon. That includes emotions." Furrowing his brows, he explained, "Your upset streaks your aura with the faintest hints of orange."

"Wow." Charon didn't know what else to say.

Immediately, Dakota settled on his knees near his head and took his hand. "That stuff stinks, by the way," he commented mildly. "What's it made out of?"

Chuckling softly, Urskin revealed, "Powdered deer penis."

"Eww," Danny mumbled, revealing that he'd returned.

Urskin barely glanced his way, saying, "It's been used in herbal medicines for centuries." Then he began a soft chant under his breath.

He was only at it for a moment when Charon caught movement in his peripheral vision. Seeing five men — four that he recognized — pulled a gasp from his throat, even though three of them he had expected. What he hadn't counted on was a visit from King Leortis himself.

"You see, your highness," Elder Gaithnos declared, pointing. "They do magick on young Charon. They've changed his features to hide him from us. We must remove him from here immediately."

The elder stood several paces to the king's right, perhaps far enough so his lies couldn't be scented. He was flanked by Glindber and Otzel. Both men appeared on edge, as if ready to sprint the fifty feet of clearing so they could grab him.

Charon knew that if they got their hands on him, there was a possibility that he would never see his mate again.

"Stay still," Dakota urged. "Let Urskin work."

"Head Enforcer Mycroft Portent," King Leortis called, slowly striding forward, the enforcer Charon didn't know flanking him. "Explain yourself." The king swept his gaze over Charon and shook his head. "Stop this unholy ritual at once."

Mycroft lifted his hands in placation as he stood to Urskin's right. "You know that we do not have the ability to cast spells on dragons, Your Highness," he stated. Indicating Charon, Mycroft claimed, "We are trying to undo a spell cast on him ten years ago." Then he pointed at Elder Gaithnos. "By the elder's order. It *was* him who convinced you a spell on Charon was necessary, after all. Wasn't it?"

To Urskin's credit, as Mycroft pled their case, the warlock never stopped casting. When he finished with the stinky cone thingy, he hurried back to the table. Charon glanced from Mycroft back to the warlock, watching him rummage through his stuff to gather . . . stuff.

"For the last ten years, Charon has been treated as a human," Mycroft continued, glaring at Gaithnos. "But being a dragon, he didn't know we had no prejudice against humans. Not like you dragons." Then he smirked at King Leortis. "No offense, of course, King Leortis. I understand you found your mate in a human a few years ago, which has changed your view . . . but many others are very slow to change. Especially with a species as long-lived as your kind." Using a hand to indicate Charon, who continued to grip Dakota as if his life depended on it, Mycroft added, "We were also ordered to keep the truth of Charon's place here a secret. Few knew he was a dragon liaison. Instead, he was a human dishwasher in our kitchens . . . for ten . . . long . . . years. Trapped in a human body, scenting as a human, and unable to take his true form . . . ever." Pointing, Mycroft stated, "By *his* orders. Isn't that right, Elder Gaithnos?"

"That is preposterous, King Leortis," Gaithnos denied vehemently. "I would never trap a dragon as a human. That would be torture. That would be—"

"A punishment," Charon cried, unable to stand listening to the elder's lies any longer. "You wanted to punish me for rejecting Glindber."

Charon remained still, refusing to move as Urskin drew symbols on his back. Noticing Glindber's narrowed eyes and flaring nostrils, he knew the dragon was losing his patience. He wanted what he wanted, and he didn't care about anything else . . . including whatever machinations his father was trying to pull off. Charon decided to push just a little bit more.

"I want to say I wish you'd just told Glindber to leave me alone and move on." Scoffing, Charon smirked at said son and egged, "But now I'm glad you didn't." Lifting his and Dakota's hands just a little, drawing attention to them, he stated, "Because of you, I've found my fated mate. We've bonded, and I'm carrying his child." Tipping his chin to the side, Charon indicated Urskin. "Once this nice warlock removes whatever curse you had that old dragon do, my life will be damn near perfect."

"No!" Glindber roared. "Charon's mine!"

An instant later, a massive red dragon reared on his hind legs, tipped his head back, and roared, flames spouting from his mouth.

"God damn it," Mycroft snapped, backing swiftly. "Egging him on so he snapped wasn't the plan."

"It worked, didn't it?" Charon countered. "He's revealing his intensions . . . and in front of the king, no less."

Except fear for those around him flooded Charon as he watched Otzel shift, too. He was a large brown dragon with a thicker body and black wings. Charon immediately worried about the damage the dragons could do.

Elder Gaithnos, on the other hand, turned into his dragon—his red scales faded with age—spread his black wings, and flew away.

"Damn it all," King Leortis hollered, pointing at the fleeing elder. "Catch the bastard."

Unfortunately, the bodyguard shook his head. "I'm sorry, my king. My duty is to your safety."

To that end, he began using his own body to back the king away from the pair of dragons that looked ready to go on a rampage at any second.

"Done," Urskin announced suddenly. "The curse is broken."

"Well fuck me," Dakota whispered, staring at Charon in shock. "You're stunning." Barking a laugh, he shook his head and grinned at Charon. "Not that you weren't before, my mate. Now, though . . ." He inhaled deeply, his nostrils flaring with open bliss. "Now . . . your human scent matches your dragon, and your outward form is gorgeous with your beautiful hazel eyes and thick auburn hair, and gods, you're just amazing."

Charon grinned at Dakota, understanding what he was saying because he suddenly found himself horny as hell. The shifter's rich masculine scent invaded his senses, making him want to wallow in the amazing aroma. He wanted to—

The roar of a dragon snapped Charon's focus back to where it needed to be—two large dragons ready to terrorize the area.

"Gotta go, my mate." Dakota pecked Charon's lips.

Then he was gone, to be replaced by a massive Komodo. He was instantly joined by two others. While Dane's Komodo appeared in equal size to Dakota's, Del was easy to tell apart . . . because he had to have at least a hundred pounds on them. That didn't seem to slow him down one bit.

The trio worked in concert. One would snap at a dragon's legs, drawing his attention. As soon as it turned, another Komodo would tear into it somewhere else. Working with them was a cheetah that sprinted around the area, lightning fast, easily evading any of the dragons' strikes. A moment later, the group was joined by a vampire, a tiger, and the biggest alligator Charon had ever seen. Even a drone zipped overhead, peppering the dragons' hide with some sort of small arms fire—probably meant more to annoy and distract than injure.

Perhaps losing patience with a ground battle, Glindber spread his wings as he set his sights on Charon. The gleam in his red eyes was clear for anyone who'd faced a dragon before to read. It was a basic dragon tactic. Fly into the sky, then swoop down, raze whatever was in their way while plucking what they wanted at the same time.

And what he wants is me.

"You're mine, omega dragon," Glindber declared as he flapped once, twice. The wind from his massive wings buffeted the shifters around him, pushing them back. "I will rip that bastard from your womb before filling you with one of my own."

Dakota's Komodo roared and lunged forward, striding against the wind as if it were nothing. He reached Glindber just as the dragon began lifting off. Opening his massive jaws, Dakota latched onto the middle of his appendage and yanked.

A pain-filled dragon-scream rent the air as Dakota tore out a huge chunk of Glindber's leathery wing.

Charon would have felt bad about it . . . if in the next instant, Glindber hadn't turned his head and blasted a stream of white-hot fire toward the house . . . where Charon knew that Miggs and Danny were hiding within.

EPILOGUE

Dakota spat out the disgusting-tasting flesh as he listened to twin hissing snarls of outrage fill the air. Turning his head, he nearly froze upon seeing the swath of dragon fire that appeared to engulf Dakota's home. Pain for his brothers almost paralyzed him, knowing that their mates had been ordered to take refuge within.

May the gods have mercy and allow them to escape out the front.

Turning his head this way and that, Dakota searched for his own mate. Except, all he saw was fire.

The thump of a tail against Dakota's side nearly sent him sprawling, but he dug his claws into the ground and slowed his slide as he glanced around to get his bearings. Roaring a warning at Dane, Dakota saw that his brother managed to yank his attention away from the house just in time to duck and avoid the heavy club at the base of the brown dragon's tail. The ground began to shake beneath their feet, and Dakota could only guess that it was a dragon causing an earthquake.

Damn it. We need these guys out of commission.

While the trees hindered the dragons' maneuverability, Dakota couldn't really see a way where it helped them, either.

Wait a minute.

Dakota spotted a tree leaning heavily, the base of the trunk having been damaged, probably by the blow of a dragon's tail. Sprinting toward it, he dug his long claws into the bark and climbed. He rocked his body, trying to send it toppling in the direction he wanted it to fall, but he couldn't seem to generate enough momentum.

Just as Dakota thought he might have to rethink his plan, a blur of spots raced up the tree past him. Then the cheetah jumped to a tree to the left, planted its paws, and lunged right back at him. Mycroft's aim was true, and he plowed into the tree just over Dakota's head and clung.

With a resounding crack, the tree began to topple.

Dakota saw the brown dragon look up at them, and it started to swing sideways. With a yank of his body in that direction—Mycroft's cheetah doing the same—they shifted the large trunk's momentum. A jolt shuddered through Dakota when they slammed the heavy trunk right on top of Otzel's head.

To Dakota's relief, Otzel dropped like a stone. In the process, Dakota and Mycroft leaped away, clearing the tangle of wings and limbs. He stumbled as he landed, the ground shaking underneath him. Except, that time, it was due to Otzel's collapse.

Turning, Dakota spotted Del and Dane standing over Glindber's downed body. Del had torn out the dragon's throat, while Dane had ripped a lengthy gash across his belly. From the unseeing dullness in Glindber's eyes, Dakota knew that the dragon was dead.

Fear that they'd managed to do it out of a grief-stricken rage flooded Dakota, and he swung his attention toward the house. After all, he could still feel his connection to his mate. Had his brothers' connections broken?

Dakota stared in confusion at what he saw. His gorgeous purple dragon lay curled up in a ball around . . . something. Beyond them, the house appeared completely intact. The only singeing seemed to be at the edge of the deck.

Easing forward, Dakota approached Charon slowly. He hiss-rumbled in worry before bumping his snout against the slightly larger beast. To his relief, he noticed the steady expand and contract of Charon's torso, telling him his mate seemed to breathe easy.

After one more bump, along with sliding his tongue over Charon's wing-scales, tasting the sweet flavor of his mate, his dragon began to move.

Charon lifted his head, uncurling it from where it had lain under his wing. "Are you okay?" he asked in his soft dragon voice — the noise rumbly and low.

Dakota nodded before bumping Charon again questioningly.

Giving him a dragon smile, Charon assured, "I'm fine. We're both fine."

Charon eased up, revealing who he covered — Urskin. The black warlock sat cross-legged on the deck. His eyes appeared vacant, and he chanted continually, but as soon as Charon moved away from him, he glanced around. He paused in whatever incantation he spoke and blew out a long breath.

"Damn," Urskin mumbled, rubbing at his chest. He smiled up at Charon. "Thank you."

"You were saving my family," Charon replied solemnly. "It was the least I could do." When Dakota cocked his head questioningly, Charon nuzzled him and explained, "Urskin be-spelled the house to repel dragon fire, but it left him unprotected. As an omega, I'm immune to dragon fire, so I curled up around him." Then Charon morphed back into his human form. Remaining on one knee, he dragged Urskin into a tight hug. "Thank you."

"You're welcome, young omega." Patting him on the shoulder before easing away, Urskin rose unsteadily to his feet. "Gonna go find that beer now," he mumbled, staggering away.

Dakota shifted and grabbed Charon, clutching him in a tight embrace. "My brave, sweet dragon," he crooned before dipping his head, intending to take his mate's mouth in a deep kiss. Turning his head at the last second, Dakota tucked

Charon close and nuzzled that spot behind his dragon's ear that he would always love. "Sorry. I can still taste that asshole's wing flesh in my mouth."

Charon chuckled as he returned the embrace. "I'll collect on that kiss later."

"Deal." Dakota lifted his head and pecked a light, closed-mouth kiss to Charon's lips. With a wink, he added, "Until later."

After his dragon smiled and nodded, Dakota glanced around and spotted Mycroft speaking animatedly with King Leortis beside the unconscious Otzel. To Dakota's relief, the grim-featured king was nodding. Dismissing them, he spotted both his brothers in similar embraces with their mates, and he smiled, relief flooding him.

Dakota returned his attention to Charon and whispered, "You saved my family. Every last damn one of us."

Charon smiled up at him so sweetly. "I saved *our* family."

Dakota nodded emphatically. "*Our* family."

A second later, Dakota found himself and Charon wrapped up in the arms of his brothers and their mates. Naked or not, they embraced, relishing their safety, freedom, and friendship.

"Our family."

ABOUT THE AUTHOR

Charlie started writing fantasy when she was eight, and after stumbling onto her first erotic romance at age nineteen, she realized her true calling. She now focuses on writing gay erotic romance, normally of the paranormal variety, with heroes of all kinds. With the help and support of her husband, Charlie finally fulfilled one of her life-long goals . . . move to acreage with her horses. You can often find her curled up with her laptop and a cup of tea or glass of wine, creating her next adventure. Charlie enjoys exploring the mountains of her new Oregon home on horseback, 4-wheeler, or motorcycle.

She can be reached at ch.richards2010@yahoo.com

Or visit her at www.charlie-richards.com.